THE WEREWOLF TYCOON'S BABY

Howls Romance

CELIA KYLE

BLURB

She thinks he's after her child, but what he really wants is... her.

For Melissa Hill, a relaxing vacation to Greece involved not only sand, but billionaire Galen Liakos as well. Their passion burned hot and bright, but when their love was threatened and their differences became painfully clear, Melissa disappeared with a hastily scribbled note.

Thank you for a wonderful vacation...

Galen Liakos is not merely a billionaire, he is the Alpha of the Liakos pack, and he is not one to be denied. Melissa is his mate, and he will have her with him once again. Non-negotiable. When he hunts her down, finding her heavily pregnant and struggling to survive, there is only one answer.

Galen will have Melissa in Greece, in his den, with his ring on her finger, and his claiming bite on her shoulder!

CHAPTER ONE

IT WAS AMAZING HOW FAST A PREGNANT WOMAN COULD run with the right motivation, and Lissa was very motivated. She bolted into the kitchen, barely avoiding one of the runners and she winced when Chef roared his displeasure.

Pregnant women do not belong in my keetchen. Go, go! Get out!

Of course, that same ornery chef slipped her a meal at the end of her shifts each night. Not one from the menu, but a dish he prepared just for her. The *bambino* needed good food to grow big and strong. Chef was a true Italian through and through.

She dipped past busy waiters and a sous chef or two as she rushed toward the back door. When she slipped past Chef, hoping that his gruff demeanor coated a good heart, she patted his back with a low apology and a few desperate words.

"Stall him. *Please*."

The swinging door to the kitchen slammed against the wall, the boom overriding the sounds in the busy kitchen.

"Lissa!" Galen's accented voice reached her and she forced herself to move faster, push harder to get free.

She shoved the back door wide, sent it swinging, and turned left toward the parking lot. The sun slowly dimmed, lessening her vision, but she could see enough to easily follow her path without tripping.

"Dammit, Lissa," he growled. Growled like the wolf that lived inside him. She knew his beast was at the surface, that running encouraged the animal to hunt her, but she couldn't help it.

She couldn't go back with him. Not after…

Lissa cupped the roundness of her stomach, hugging the precious cargo she carried. She couldn't let him get ahold of her. Not after all she'd heard, not after all she'd experienced in Greece.

"Lissa!" His roar wrapped around her.

Yeah, Galen was pretty pissed. Yet another reason she couldn't let him catch her.

The crunch of his expensive Italian shoes on the uneven gravel-covered ground of the alley told her how close he was to catching her. That couldn't happen, not while she had breath in her body and life in her veins. She had too much to live for, too much to protect. The child in her womb rolled, seeming to stretch and press against the confines of her body. It was as if the baby knew his father was near. For all she knew, that was exactly right. She didn't know much about werewolves, the world didn't know much about werewolves, but she definitely knew about Galen Liakos. And she knew he wasn't one to take losing with grace.

And that was what he'd done. He branded her with his body, and then she discovered the truth. The truth that made her leave him with hardly a second glance and nothing more than the clothes on her back, a small bit of cash, and her passport.

The rumble of a familiar bus reached her and she nearly stopped in relief. It was pure luck, as if the bus gods took pity on her and read her mind. As she rounded the last corner of the building, she nearly skidded on the uneven ground but managed to catch herself by grasping the brick wall. Her nails grated against the rough surface, and the sting of pain told her she'd broken more than one. But that small hurt didn't matter, not compared to keeping her baby from harm. Still cupping her belly, she raised her hand and waved to get the bus driver's attention.

"Wait! Please, wait!" Lissa met the driver's gaze, pleading with him with her eyes, and begging him to wait just one more second.

She could practically feel Galen breathing down her neck, his scent enveloping her in a seductive blanket. But she couldn't succumb to his charms once again. She had to think of someone other than herself now. A small life she loved more than anyone she'd ever known depended on her and she refused to let her child down.

The bus remained in place, the door wide and waiting for her, and she dug deep, snatching up what strength she could and pushed herself harder. It took her one giant leap to finally dash into the old vehicle, and the moment she was within its confines, she begged to the driver once again. "Shut the door! Shut it before he gets in! Please!"

She wasn't sure whether it was the hysterical tone of her voice or the pure terror in her expression, but something had the man behind the wheel following her order without hesitation. The double doors slammed shut a bare moment before Galen collided with the side of the bus. Large fists pounded on the metal and glass, and she wondered how much abuse they could take before they shattered and granted the werewolf entrance. The bus' engine roared to life, the rumble overpowering the sound of Galen's snarls and growls. The man glaring at her through the glass was not the one she'd spent two blissful weeks with all of those months ago. No, this was the ruthless businessman, the unforgiving head of the Liakos family, the Liakos pack Alpha, and president of Liakos Holdings.

He bared his fangs, pulling back his lips and flashing his elongated canines. Fur lined his cheeks, and his eyes were the unmistakable yellow of his inner wolf. In that moment he was pure alpha, pure dominance, and purely pissed... at her.

The bus slowly gathered speed as the driver ran it through its gears and demanded the massive vehicle respond. The entire time, Galen kept pace, his glare focused entirely on her as he ran. Lissa hadn't feared him in Greece, not when she'd discovered he was a billionaire nor when she found out he was a werewolf. Even discovering he was an alpha hadn't frightened her. But right then, right there, she was deathly afraid. Afraid for herself—she rubbed her stomach, attempting to soothe the child still within her—afraid for her baby.

They continued their rapid race down the street, the surrounding cityscape passing with an ever-increasing speed, until the world around them was nearly a blur.

And still Galen kept pace with them. At least until two other large bodies came abreast with his racing form and tackled him to the ground, ceasing his pursuit. His bodyguards. They went everywhere with him. At first it'd been a novelty, something that annoyed her but her love for him overshadowed those feelings. Now, she was truly thankful the men were at hand. They were good at their jobs and never let Galen out of their sight. In his current condition, with his anger riding him hard, Galen would have chased the bus no matter the risk to himself. Wolves liked a good chase…

Snarls erupted on the street, and she knew he battled with the two other males. They wouldn't be able to hold him down for long—even two against one. He was the Alpha for a reason. But for now, she had some breathing room. With a sigh, she relaxed against the grime caked bus floor. She had no idea what coated the ground, but she had more important things to think about. Such as her escape. She didn't know how he'd found her, she just knew that she had to disappear once again.

"Are you okay, miss?" The driver's voice was deep and caring yet tinged with unease.

Lissa swallowed hard, and forced herself to push aside the rising panic. "I'm-I'm fine. Just," she took a deep calming breath. "Just an ex-boyfriend."

"Looks like it's a good thing he's an ex. I don't normally

have problems with those wolves, but that one," he shook his head, "that one looks like trouble."

Trouble? That was one way to look at her relationship with Galen.

Deadly was another.

Lissa remained in place, catching her breath after that mad dash. She'd get up soon. When her heart no longer fought to burst from her chest.

The bus driver glanced in his rearview mirror, and then turned his attention back to her for a brief moment. "I can't see him anymore. Why don't you go ahead and slide onto that seat there?"

It was a question, but more like an order. One she was more than happy to abide. With a groan she heaved herself to her feet, grasping a nearby pole to steady herself before finally settling onto one of the benches. She ignored the stares, the questions that lingered in other passengers' eyes and the hateful glances shot her way. It was always that way in the larger cities. In places where wolves were less likely to congregate. Suburbia and small towns accepted werewolves without a problem. They were used to seeing them on two feet and four throughout the years. Inner cities, however...

"Miss?" The driver drew her attention and she focused on the kind, large man.

"Yes," she nodded, "he's a lot of trouble."

"Is there somewhere I can drop you that's safe? There's a shelter on my route..."

A shelter. Yes, that'd be a good place to hide, to keep away from Galen while she figured out where to run next. The baby rolled and pressed against her, kicking her stomach as if in protest. She rubbed the bulge with a soft murmur. It was as if the child knew her thoughts and protested her desire to continue running.

She'd been running for months. How long now? Six months? Seven? The first night she'd given herself to Galen, she'd become pregnant, losing her virginity and gaining a child in one passionate act. When she'd woken that next morning, it was to find a beaming Galen looming over her, a wide smile splitting his lips. "Good morning, *agapi mou*. You have made me the happiest wolf alive." He traced the line of her nose with a single finger and then tapped the end. "When you are prepared, we will rise and make our announcement to the pack."

She'd furrowed her brow, confusion filling her. "What announcement?"

Galen ran his hand down her abdomen and finally stopping when he reached her lower stomach. "That you carry the future of the Liakos pack."

And that had been the beginning of the end.

"Miss?"

The past had a way of drawing her in. Lissa shook her head, banishing those thoughts. "No," she needed to settle this mess. "I'll get off at the stop by my house."

She couldn't avoid Galen forever. Definitely not now that he'd found her. It was time to stop running and time to make a stand. He may rule the Liakos pack in Greece, but his title and status meant nothing in the U.S. She could confront him, and then send him on his way. There was nothing he could do to her here. At least, she hoped not. Because it was no longer just her life at stake, but also the life of her child. Galen's Alpha bitch had made that more than clear.

You are safe for now because you carry his child. But the moment you do not, you will be discarded.

All too soon the air brakes on the bus whistled and thumped as they slowed the vehicle, and it rolled to a gentle stop at the all-too-familiar bus stop. She gave the driver a grateful smile, hoping to banish the frown from his lips and wasn't surprised when it remained firmly in place.

"I'm not so sure about this, miss."

"Everything will be fine." Even she didn't believe her own words.

Without a second glance, she carefully made her way

down the steps and steadied herself when her feet finally rested on the sidewalk. The further along she got in her pregnancy, the harder it was to move around and retain her balance. The baby wiggled and stretched inside her, reminding her of his presence, and she gently rested her hand atop her roundness. "We'll be home soon, little pup."

Her home, not Galen's. That was something she needed to keep at the forefront of her mind and remind Galen of when they finally had their confrontation.

She slowly waddled toward home, forcing a smile to her face as she passed the park and waved at the children calling out to her. She often spent afternoons there, watching the little ones play and laugh, as she hoped her child would someday. Not stopping, she drew nearer to her apartment. It wasn't long before she was gripping the handrail of the stairs and carefully making her way up the steps to the second floor. She dug in her purse, easily finding her house keys, but before she could slip the key inside the lock, the door was wrenched open.

And there he was, Galen Liakos, the man she'd run from for so long.

Olive skin, midnight hair, strong features and heavily muscled body... all so familiar. Even the gray fur that peppered his flesh and the yellowed eyes that overtook the normal chocolate hues were familiar. She knew his body almost as well as she knew her own. They'd touched, tasted, and loved each other for two weeks before it all came crashing down. And now he was back. Would he destroy her all over again?

Probably.

Fury coated his features, and she knew it was only a matter of time before his roars echoed off the walls. Rather than causing the spectacle in the middle of the hallway, she brushed past him and carefully made her way into her home.

"Galen," she murmured as she passed.

Lissa didn't miss his growl.

She would brave this out. She would explain her position, tell him exactly what would happen, and then he would leave.

"Melissa," he snarled her name.

She ignored the violence in his tone and looked around her small apartment, noting its apparent emptiness. "Where are Stavros and Leo?"

"Leave others out of this mess! Do not say another man's name in my presence!"

So very, very Greek.

Galen wasn't done. "You will get your things and you will leave with me right now. This game is through."

Lissa fought the nerves that threatened to make her tremble before him. "I wasn't aware I've been playing a game. I left you, Galen. I left you and returned to the U.S."

More fur coated his skin, sliding down his arms and onto his hands. "With *my* child."

"No," she rested both hands on her stomach, "with *my* child."

Pure rage filled his features and his cheekbones sharpened, the low snap of bones easily heard in the suppressing quiet of the room. "Melissa, it is only because we shared so much that my beast has not attacked. You have disobeyed my orders and kidnapped the next Liakos pack Alpha and my heir. Any other wolf in my pack would be dead by now."

Lissa gasped and tightened her hold on her stomach as she backed away from Galen's intimidating presence. "You don't mean that."

"I do. Without question."

"I saved this baby from hell at your hands."

His features tightened and his body seemed to grow in size. His shoulders widening, muscles increasing, hands slowly transforming into claws. She took another step back, putting more space between them. Not that the increased separation would truly protect her. Nothing would shield her from an alpha bent on destruction.

"Our history and that child are why you're still breathing. The fact that you are not familiar with our culture is also staying my hand. Do not mistake this hesitancy as weakness." His chest expanded as he breathed deeply, and when he exhaled, his size seemed to lessen slightly. "There is no reason to fear me. *Now*. There are many things to discuss, and there is still much time before you give birth to devise how to handle things going forward." Another deep breath. "Now, gather your things. We will leave within the hour."

She shook her head. "I'm not going anywhere with you, Galen."

"Yes, you are. I will not have my orders questioned by you once again." He was so unforgiving, so unbendable, which was yet another reason she refused to go with him.

"No." There wasn't much more for her to say. Excuses and justifications weren't anything amidst Galen's overwhelming power. So nothing else was worth saying.

The yellow in his eyes overtook any hint of humanity

within him. "I do not think you understand your position, *agapi mou*. You carry my child and that child will be born in Greece surrounded by his pack. That is the way every Liakos Alpha came into this world and my child will be no different!"

"And I don't think you realize we're in the United States. I am a U.S. citizen, and my baby will be born here. Unless you're willing to start an international-interspecies incident by kidnapping me."

"Like you kidnapped my own pup?"

Fury filled her, the emotion fueled by the constant fear that had dogged her heels for so long. "I did not kidnap my own baby. I *saved* him. Why can't you understand that? How can you so callously throw away his life?"

Galen pressed his lips together, forming a white slash across his face, and a rolling growl filled the room. "I will pretend I did not hear those words from your mouth. You are the mother of my child, and you are pregnant, so much will be forgiven. But do not think for one moment that your behavior can continue. I cannot and will not allow your constant insubordination."

Lissa snorted. "You act as if you'll be in my presence long enough for me to continue acting this way when that is just not going to happen. You're leaving without me. That's all there is to it. Because I refuse to allow my baby to be pulled into your violent, hate filled world. A child needs love and safety and he wouldn't find either with the Liakos pack. With you."

A new emotion flickered across his features so quickly that she wasn't sure what she'd seen. It was there and gone from one heartbeat to the next. "Regardless of your feelings, that doesn't change the fact you carry my heir and you will return to Greece with me. Immediately."

A bone deep lethargy overwhelmed her, sinking into her body and dragging her down. She'd been working so hard these past months, spending hour upon hour on her feet so she could save money to support herself after the baby's birth. Now, being so close to Galen, and fighting with him, sapped her of what little strength she still held. She just had to hold on a little longer, remain on her feet a few more minutes. Once she got him out of her apartment, she could fall to pieces. But not a moment sooner.

"And regardless of your feelings, I am not returning to Greece. I'm staying right here and having my baby at the hospital down the street. Nothing you say or do will make me change my mind. Are you so heartless that you make me return to a place I hate?"

His expression remained firm and unshakable. "Yes."

"Galen," she leaned against the wall, catching her weight with first her hand, and then she leaned against the firm surface. The tiredness continued to pull it her, as darkness crept into her vision.

No, not now.

"Galen," she squeezed her eyes shut tight and battled to push the urge to faint back. "I am-"

"Melissa?"

"I am not—" She was losing the fight as the darkness wrapped around her in a cloying blanket.

"Melissa?" Galen's voice was hoarse and thin.

She didn't want him near her, didn't want to depend on him once again, but she hoped he was still human enough to care for their child. "Don't take him from me, please. Please don't take him. He's all I have left. Please..."

The last thing she saw before unconsciousness took her was a brief flash of worry.

Galen, worried? Never. Then again, she was carrying his heir. She mustn't forget the heir. After all, the Alpha bitch wasn't going to.

CHAPTER TWO

Lissa wasn't sure what to expect when she woke, but it sure as hell wasn't to find herself flying across the ocean in Galen's private jet. The interior was well known to her, with its slick surfaces and plush leather seating. The soft carpet always gave way beneath her bare feet, and she had more than one good memory of flying the skies with Galen at her side. He'd introduced her to so much in so little a time, and it'd only taken a few choice—and deadly—words to end the fairytale. Well, it was gone but he seemed intent on dragging her back into his world.

She carefully glanced around the room, closing her eyes when dizziness overtook her. She didn't need to see in order to know Galen was nearby. His scent permeated everything around her, and it was clear he'd been at her side very recently. Gathering what little strength she had, she forced her lids to part once again and she blinked against the brightness that invaded her eyes.

The low murmur of voices reached her and she grimaced, recognizing not just Galen's, but Stavros, Leo, and Dr. Martin—one of the pack doctors—as well. It was not long before the voices rose while snarls and growls were interjected between words. That was the way Galen communicated. He had no idea how to simply speak with someone. His wolf always got the better of him. She was glad to know he wasn't just saving his bad temper for her.

"... must remain calm." The doctor's words were probably meant to be soothing, but fell short of the mark.

"You dare lecture me on calm? I am calm!"

Yeah, he was totally calm.

"You must think of the child, Alpha." Again the tone was comforting.

Lissa didn't need to see the change in Galen's appearance. She felt it in the air. It vibrated through the entire plane, sliding into her flesh and sinking into her bones. His wolf was out in full force, and had been looking for a target. He couldn't come after *her*, so it seemed the doctor would receive the brunt of his anger.

A single gasp told her she was right. The doctor knew better than to push his Alpha when the man was so on edge. Or rather, he did not.

A soft whimper slid past the doorway and she realized that not just Dr. Martin was being forced to submit, but it seemed the other two males as well. And because of her. Swallowing her fear, she swung her feet over the edge of the bed and pushed herself up until she sat on the edge. Another look at her surroundings revealed she was in the bedroom she'd once shared with Galen. They'd made love more than once on this small surface. Was it intentional that he laid her to rest there? Or was a simple coincidence?

No, he'd done it on purpose. The man didn't do anything without careful planning.

She pushed to her feet and shuffled toward the door, grasping the knob with one hand while clutching the frame with the other as she swung the panel wide. And she found exactly what she anticipated. Dr. Martin, Stavros, and Leo, as well as the flight attendant whose name she could not remember kneeling on the plush floor of the plane. Each one had their head tilted to the side, baring their neck for their Alpha. She leaned against the frame, hard-won strength already leeching away due to those small movements.

"Galen," she whispered his name with a small breath.

It took that barely there sound to get his attention, and he swung his yellow-eyed gaze to her. The orbs bore into her, as if sinking into her soul. He weighed her and she couldn't figure out if he found her worthy or lacking. His expression did not change, his bearing remaining rigid and firm. Did she see a small flicker in his expression? A hint at the compassion and caring they once shared?

No. Never from him. It had never been there to begin with, had it?

"Save your anger for me. Don't take our problems out on them."

He narrowed his eyes, glaring at her, weighing her once again. "You would defend my own wolves to me? Do they seem like children to you to need a woman to hide behind?"

Lissa swallowed the first words that sprung to her lips, and instead said, "No, I merely point out that they are not the reason for your bad humor. They've done nothing but support you and stand beside you. I'm simply trying to make you see their worth as more than verbal punching bags."

Galen tightened his lips slightly, and yet another emotion slid through his eyes for the barest moment before his face was shuttered once again. "So, I should use you instead?"

She could no longer hold his gaze and instead tore her eyes from him to stare out one of the windows. There was nothing but a sea of blue with soft splashes of white clouds that occasionally sped by.

"Yes," she snapped.

"I would dare not turn this rage onto a female." His words were harsh but filled with truth.

No, you would simply give the task to the Alpha bitch.

"That doesn't change the fact they don't deserve this treatment." She still wouldn't look at him.

"Stavros and Leo allowed you to escape, doesn't that deserve a certain amount of punishment?"

Lissa cut him a glance. "I'm sure you've done enough at this point, but it wasn't Stavros and Leo who allowed me to get away from you. That person is beyond even your reach."

And she'd never reveal the name of the kind old man who'd met her in the dead of night and driven her to the docks. He was human and sympathetic since he knew of a wolf's violent nature.

"You're so sure he's beyond me?"

Of course she was. She wouldn't have involved anyone who would suffer for involving themselves in her life. It was why she hadn't depended on anyone. Not truly.

"Yes."

Galen's attention snapped to the three kneeling men and single female. "You're dismissed."

All four slowly rose to their feet, the flight attendant the first to scamper away and retreat to the front of the plane. Stavros and Leo carefully made their way back to the seating area they typically claimed. It was only the doctor who seemed brave enough to remain in place.

"Alpha?" The male's voice wasn't hesitant in the least.

"What?" A snarl was on Galen's lips.

"The bearing one?"

The bearing one. Couldn't the physician even say her name? She was basically being referred to as the incubator. Nice.

Galen returned his attention to her. "Have you been seen by a physician?"

"Of course." As if she'd endanger her child.

"One that specializes in werewolves?"

Lissa snapped her jaw shut, refusing to answer the question.

"I thought not." Galen gestured toward Dr. Martin. "He

will attend you since your examinations have been lacking."

She had no response to that autocratic statement and instead met the doctor's gaze. "I'm ready whenever you are."

Despite the circumstances, she was looking forward to being examined by a werewolf physician. She knew mixed pregnancies were different than traditional humans, but she hadn't had a werewolf doctor at her disposal. If she'd approached a pack, they would've demanded the name of the sire, and that was something she refused to reveal.

"*We* are ready." Galen was as demanding and arrogant as ever.

She kept her mouth shut, refusing to rise to the bait, and merely followed Dr. Martin as he moved toward one of the other rooms on the plane. It was a guestroom, one that looked like the other two the plane housed. Or was it?

Small changes were made, the bed had been swapped out, and new cabinets lined one wall. Even the flooring had been torn up and replaced. She catalogued all these modifications, wondering why Galen had gone to the expense to make this room so much different. It wasn't less luxurious, but there was something...

"I had the alterations ordered the moment we discovered your pregnancy. I also contracted the doctor to travel with us during this time. Your care will be shared between Dr. Martin and my brother." His gaze bore into her, the yellow and brown warring, and it wasn't just anger that filled his features now; there was affection with a heavy dose of desire. "I wanted the plane to be prepared should anything happen to you during our travels. You see, I didn't want to be away from you for even a moment, but I also couldn't stand the thought of putting you or our child at risk. The technology contained within this room rivals that of the best hospital in the world." His expression darkened, those hints of desire she glimpsed banished by a renewed rage. "Which you would have known had you stayed. You would have known how much I cared for you and our child. You would have known how much you were cherished."

Lissa looked around the room, seeing it with new eyes and noticed what the luxury kept hidden. She replayed his words in her mind, searching for any hidden meaning behind each syllable, and only had one thought. "Were?"

"Were." Past tense. No longer cherished. The word was flat, and no emotion lived in the tone.

Quiet reigned, and she wondered what was expected of her now. The soft rustle of cloth, the quiet shift of the doctor's weight from one foot to the other, reminded them both they were not alone. Galen's attention snapped from her to the doctor. "What tests need to be done?"

Dr. Martin bustled into action, pulling open cabinets and repositioning the bed. In moments familiar equipment was in place and she recognized the sonogram machine. The bed was tilted and angled and moved into position before he finally turned his attention to her. "If the bearing one would please take a seat here."

She went into action, used to these types of visits by now. Her human doctor knew her child was of mixed race so Lissa got quite a few more ultrasounds than the average pregnant mother. Within seconds of reclining on the seat, she lifted her maternity shirt and then carefully lowered her pants, baring the large mound of her stomach. When the doctor's gaze landed on her bared body, Galen released a low, rumbling growl. One cut off barely a second after it began. She turned her shocked gaze to him, but was met with another one of his blank, unemotional expressions. But, the sound was not lost on the physician.

His hand shook as he squirted the cool gel on her bare skin and her quick intake of breath was then echoed by yet another growl from the man at her side. She didn't bother turning her attention to Galen, she knew what she'd see and she wasn't prepared to meet yet another blank stare. Where his smiles used to be plentiful and freely given, he now seemed to only frown when he looked upon her. Or worse, did nothing at all.

"This is a bit cool." The doctor's voice trembled, and she gave him a gentle smile.

"Yes, I'm used to this part." She tried to put them at ease, but her words seem to only serve to cause him to shake harder, so she kept her mouth shut.

It took no time for him to begin his task of performing the ultrasound, the wand sliding over her hot flesh with ease as he examined her child. The rapid thump of her baby's heartbeat filled the small area, and she smiled at the healthy, rapid pace. The baby squirmed and twisted inside her, seeming to shy away from the doctor's movements. When it yet again twisted away, Lissa couldn't suppress her chuckle.

"He always does that. He doesn't like ultrasounds all that much."

The doctor froze in place, as if sensing danger, and it was Galen who broke the stillness.

"He? We are having a son?"

Lissa jolted and shot a look at the man at her side. "I don't know for sure. He was never in the right position, but I couldn't call my child an 'it,' could I?"

"You could have called *our* child many things had you

merely stayed at my side. You could have been monitored every step of this pregnancy had you remained at my side. I could know how you'd react to an ultrasound if you had stayed at my side!" His voice rose with every statement until his shout echoed off the room's walls.

While the doctor seemed to tremble at Galen's rising volume, Lissa did anything but. Instead, she met him —murderous glare for murderous glare. "And how long would I have been at your side after I gave birth to your heir? Five minutes? Ten minutes? Would you have even let me hold him before you *disposed* of me?"

The yellow in his eyes seemed to glow even in the bright light of the room, and gray fur rapidly coated his face, sliding down his neck, and disappearing beneath his shirt. "As if I would ever harm the mother of my child. Better wolves would die for the insult you just gave me."

"It's a good thing I'm not one of your wolves then isn't it? I assume if I was, you'd simply drag me into the middle of the woods, cut the pup for my stomach, and leave me for the natural wolves then." Lissa didn't try to suppress the sneer that leapt to her lips. She didn't believe him for a second.

"It was not long ago that passion wasn't fueled by anger, *agapi mou*." He reached for her, and traced the line of her cheek with a single claw-tipped finger.

She hated him. She had every reason to run. Her actions had been justified. It was dangerous to remain at his side. And yet... When he looked at her in that way, when he touched her so gently despite his rampaging wolf, she wanted him. Her body was anxious to be taken by him, and immediately her nipples pebbled and hardened within her bra. She ached deep inside herself, her entire being anxious to be possessed by him once again. Oh, why had she not run when she had the chance? She knew it would take one kiss, one caress, and she would be back under his control again. She had no strength when it came to Galen. None at all. No self-respect, no conviction, and no power to resist him.

She tore away from him and jerked her attention to the ultrasound monitor. "Seven months, Galen seven months ago that was true." She turned to him. "It is no longer."

Lissa held his gaze, refusing to back down. He was an alpha through and through, but once upon a time, she thought she was strong enough to stand at his side and rule the pack with him. Well, she wasn't prepared to run the Liakos pack, but she did want to prove that she wasn't one of his weak wolves. The confrontation continued, silence stretching longer, but she didn't give up. She would win this single confrontation. Just one.

The doctor settled the matter between them. "Alpha, please. This is not good for the child."

With a grim frown, Galen's attention returned to the ultrasound monitor. "Is the child okay?"

"Yes," Dr. Martin repositioned the wand, pressed down, and typed a few keys. "You can see here that the pregnancy is progressing as normal for a mixed species birth. The measurements are as anticipated. He is a strong boy and will be big like his papa."

Galen asked the same question as moments ago. "He?"

The doctor glanced at her and then gave Galen his full attention. "Yes, Alpha, you are having a boy."

A boy. She was going to have a little boy. He would have his father's olive skin and dark hair. He'd probably have his father's autocratic attitude as well. A pang pierced her heart. She only wished that she'd be around to teach him gentleness and caring to offset the violence of the werewolf world. If only...

"My heir..." Galen whispered two words, and she turned her head toward him. "I will never forgive you for denying me this."

Lissa didn't doubt he meant the words. There was no denying the anger that radiated from his body. And she understood the source of his rage. Any other male, human or werewolf, would feel the same. And yet, she would have behaved exactly as she had if she had to do it all over again. No, she would've hidden better, she would've run farther, and she would've sought more help. Anything if it meant keeping her baby away from the Liakos pack, away from Galen.

"I understand."

"Do you?" Breath rasped in and out of his lungs, the whispered sound battling against the rapid thrum of their child's heartbeat. "You understand what it's like to fall asleep with my mate in my arms, our child protected in her womb, only to awaken alone in a cold bed?" He stared at her, glared at her and she found she could not tear her gaze from his. "You understand what it's like to think my only chance at happiness had been stolen and destroyed by my enemies? You understand what it's like to grieve for what you had for so short a time and then suddenly lost?"

The truth of her actions, the effect her disappearance had on him, was unmistakable. And she was almost lulled into feeling guilty for a brief moment. Almost made to regret her actions.

And then she remembered...

You are safe for now because you carry his child. But the moment you do not, you will be discarded.

The true question was did he understand what it was

like to grieve for a future that would forever be denied her?

She opened her mouth to put voice to those words, but the plane chose that moment to tremble and jar them. It was enough to break their colliding gazes and he looked to Dr. Martin. "Is the child healthy? Is he okay?" As the doctor nodded, he continued speaking. "Then the rest of the examination can wait until we've landed. For now you should both secure yourselves for our arrival."

Galen strode toward the room's only door, and it was then that she finally found her voice. "Where are we? Where are we landing?"

The large, imposing male, stopped in the doorway and turned back to her. "Where you belong, where you have always belonged. Greece."

CHAPTER THREE

LISSA CUPPED THE ROUNDNESS OF HER PREGNANT BELLY as if her hand could protect the child within from the barely suppressed violence surrounding her. She didn't need a werewolf within her to sense the low growls that trailed her through the Liakos pack house. No, they weren't audible, but even in the short time she was with Galen she could now recognize the subtle vibrations of a werewolf's chest.

They couldn't hate her more than she hated herself. She'd tried to protect her son. Tried and failed. And now she was back where she'd started. A lamb thrown to the wolves.

Lissa padded past the guard stationed by the front door, ignoring the way his bright yellow eyes followed her every move and the sneer that graced his lips. He didn't want her there? She didn't want to be there.

They were even. She slipped into one of her favorite rooms in the house, the large and open space with windows that looked over the tumultuous sea. A well-worn path led from the house toward the ocean. She knew that course well. She would laugh and play, race from the massive home over the hard, packed ground, down the natural steps that had been carved into the cliff face and then once she hit the sand at the base it was a quick dash into the water. All the while, Galen would be on her heels, playfully barking and snapping at her in a mock chase.

Happy memories. Happy times. At least until she'd become pregnant. Become a threat.

The low clearing of a throat garnered her attention, and she slowly turned toward the room's entry. Slowly. Everything had to be done slowly now. Not just because of her large stomach, but she feared the pack's response to sudden movements. They were excited by the chase, excited at the prospect of pouncing. She was sure there was more than one pack member who'd love nothing more than to take her down.

But not before the baby is born. I can't forget that. I'm useful until then, useful and safe.

She met Leo's gaze. "Hello, Leo. Nice to see you again."

It was a lie. She knew he could smell the lie. But she'd been raised with manners.

Leo grunted but did not reply to her greeting. "Alpha requested I escort you to dinner."

Dinner. Lissa looked down her body, glancing at her maternity pants and flowery top. Not exactly glitz and glamour dinner wear. And the Liakos pack "dressed" for dinner. "Very well." She moved toward him, waddling and carefully navigating around the scattered the furniture. "Lead the way."

She and Galen hadn't ever used the dining room during her brief stay. More often than not, they ate in bed and when they weren't tangled in the sheets, they were at some of the city's most exclusive restaurants.

Leo raised the single brow in question. "In that?"

The sneer was in his tone, but she was beyond caring. Her polite greeting was the last of her reserves and all that remained were anger and fear. "If your *Alpha* wanted me in an evening gown, he would have bought me one. You're not questioning your Alpha, are you?"

He narrowed his eyes, the yellow flaring with his anger. No werewolf, especially the males, liked being questioned. Well, neither did pregnant women.

"Of course, he did not," a familiar feminine voice interrupted their conversation. "One of the Alpha's most trusted guards would never dream of questioning Galen," Andrea—the Liakos Alpha bitch—purred as she slunk past Leo. Some Alpha bitches were mated to the Alpha while some were not. In the Liakos pack, Andrea wasn't. "I didn't realize Galen sent you on this errand." Andrea wrinkled her nose. "I was coming to fetch Melissa myself." She waved her fingers at the larger wolf. "We'll be right behind you."

Leo narrowed his eyes for a brief moment, his attention flicking from Lissa to Andrea and back again. Did he see her fear? Her rising panic at the thought of being alone with Andrea? Had her scent grown stronger and more pronounced with her increased panic? She prayed the answer to those questions was yes. She prayed he would remain and protect her from Andrea. She nearly snorted aloud. Why should she expect help from any of the Liakos pack when the Alpha was happy to discard her?

"Run along," Andrea snapped at Leo and he carefully retreated, not turning his back until he was out of sight. Smart wolf. The Alpha bitch tilted her head to the side, as if listening to Leo's retreat, and then the smile she'd been sporting since entering the room turned evil. It was filled with the promise of pain and retribution and Lissa knew what the female had in mind.

She'd told her, after all.

... carve... heart...throat...

"That was not smart you stupid, stupid girl." Andrea

wrapped her fingers around Lissa's bicep and her wolf's nails dug into her flesh. "Do you understand the problems you've caused?" She tightened her grip further. "I can't plan the mating ceremony until this business is handled. He can think of nothing but your stupid mongrel brat. You better not run again, bitch."

Through it all, she kept her lips shut, refusing to utter a sound. It was what the twisted female wanted. She wanted to hear Lissa cry and whine with the pain. Wanted her to shout for assistance just so she could be shown the power the Alpha bitch held. That first time all those months ago, her first violent interaction with Andrea had ended with a concerned Stavros rushing into the room she and Andrea occupied. He was a skilled guard, his gaze encompassed the situation in one sweep. He'd seen Lissa on her knees, bleeding and gasping for air while Andrea stood over her, that same blood dripping from her claws. She called out to Stavros once again, but a quickly barked order from Andrea had him disappearing.

As demonstrations went, it was effective. The message had been clear. Lissa was nothing, Lissa's words meant nothing. Even when she'd gone to Galen with her concerns and tears in her eyes, her worries and problems had been brushed aside.

"I have spoken with Andrea about this. It is good she was

there to assist you when you fell. I am only sorry she pricked to with her claws. Here, I shall kiss them better."

He'd gone on to kissing all of her, his lips gliding over every inch of her skin and exploring her body until all worries about Andrea and the pack were banished. It'd been glorious. A night of lovemaking she wouldn't soon forget for more than one reason. He'd made love to her in so many ways until she'd been brought to tears.

Andrea squeezed even tighter and Lissa sucked in a quick, harsh breath. Her child twisted and turned inside her stomach in response to her pain, the baby always conscious of her emotions and feelings. She dropped her free hand to her belly, trying to fight back the pain as well as sooth the little boy.

"Do you hear me? Don't run again."

Lissa spoke through gritted teeth. "I heard you."

With her agreement, Andrea released her and pushed her away, making Lissa stumble. "Good. Now come along. He's holding dinner for you."

A hand pressed to the wounds on her arm, she straightened and followed the Alpha bitch. They padded down the hallways, her bare feet sinking into the plush carpet, and as they neared the entry to the dining room, Lissa reached over and plucked a pristine white cloth napkin from a table placed just outside the doors. Wolves were messy and had hair trigger tempers. It was why they had an entire eight-foot table loaded with extra napkins silverware and dinnerware at the ready.

She pressed it to her arm, swallowing the moan of pain that threatened to escape, and continued on her path. Everyone fell silent at their entry—because of Andrea or Lissa?—and Lissa ignored their heavy stares. A low growl, loud enough for Lissa to hear, sent a tendril of unease down her spine. That the sound continued until Galen released a furious whip of Greek and the offender dropped his shoulders, tilted his head to the side, and whimpered in response.

As soon as they were within ten feet of the head of the table where Galen sat, Andrea broke out in apologies. "I'm so sorry we're late, darlin—" she coughed. "I mean Alpha."

An accidental slip of the tongue or intentional? Who knew? Who cared?

Lissa. She cared because even though she didn't want to be around him, didn't want their child raised in this environment, she loved a part of him.

"Dear Melissa stumbled and needed a moment to collect herself." Andrea glanced back at her, those eyes wide and guileless. "Oh, dear. Did I prick you? I'm so sorry." Andrea looked to Galen. "She's so clumsy. It was just like the last time she was here."

Andrea was a sneaky bitch that was for sure. In a handful of words, she was able to blame Lissa's injuries on herself as well as remind the Alpha of the fact that she'd run from him. She plastered a smile on her lips and continued on, moving past the smug bitch and toward the empty chair at Galen's right. The chair she'd occupied when she was last here. True, they'd never dined with others, but she naturally assumed that was where she would sit once again.

It wasn't until she reached for the chair that Galen spoke to her. "You'll sit at my left."

The words struck her, reminding her once again of her place. She'd forgotten for a moment, forgotten the significance of being in that seat. His right hand. The one he could depend on for support above all others.

Not her.

"Of course." She glided around him as if it didn't matter and Stavros was there to pull out her chair.

"Are you well?" She focused on him and noted his attention on her arm. She pulled the bloodied napkin away, and was gratified to see that the wounds were on their way to being healed. It would take time, but not nearly as much as a normal human. She was no longer normal. She was pregnant with a werewolf pup and he took care of his mother.

"Yes. Andrea is right, it was a repeat." A small movement drew her attention to the man standing behind Galen. Stavros. Stavros with his eyes widening for a moment and then narrowing as he focused on Andrea. She wasn't going to say more, not in front of the pack, but Andrea wouldn't quit.

"She's so clumsy, Alpha. I do hope your child does not inherit that *human* trait." The way she said human was just shy of a sneer.

"Coincidentally, the only time I've had difficulties like this is here." Her voice was flat. "Somehow I'm capable of carrying a thirty pound tray of food in one hand, a carafe of sparkling water in the other, and pour drinks as I make my way around the restaurant serving food."

"Of course. But you're so..." the woman curled her lips slightly, "large."

"Why don't you ask your Alpha what I was doing when he found me?" Galen sucked in a harsh breath and she shot him a glance to see the fury coating his features, but she was more concerned in winning this battle with Andrea. He was more than a little pissed that she'd chosen waitressing and working long hours over staying with him in the lap of luxury. The woman's wolf was present, those eyes yellow and fierce. Lissa consumed herself with folding the bloodied napkin into a small square and then carefully laid it atop the pristine tablecloth. "As I said. The issue might be the location."

Galen's attention swung to the bloodied fabric, his stare hot and intent and it was only broken when Stavros stepped forward to murmur in his ear. The words were low, but had an immediate effect on Galen as well as Andrea. The Alpha's expression softened and he nodded while Andrea's seemed too harden further.

He reached for her hand, gathering her fingers in his and resting their twined hands on the red cloth. He lifted his head and stared out at those gathered around the long table. Easily thirty of the highest ranking Liakos pack wolves were in the room, and he looked to them all. "Then we shall do our best to make this a safe place for you and our child."

The words seemed innocuous, but the hardness in his tone revealed it was an order. Yes, the Alpha was furious with her, but he wanted her safe. Or rather, he wanted his child safe. At the moment Lissa was simply the incubator.

He carefully withdrew his hold, seemingly satisfied with the warning he imparted, and waved to one of the nearby servers to begin the meal. The wolf approached, tray laden with various meats that appealed to a beast's need for nearly raw protein. From behind her, someone reached around and carefully placed a beautifully prepared plate that included some of her favorite vegetables and fully cooked chicken. Her baby immediately revolted, pushing and prodding her from the inside, and she knew the child's problem.

Shaking her head, she carefully placed her fingertips on the server's arm to stop his retreat. The second a familiar growl hit the air, she snatched her hand back. The last thing she wanted was Galen going after this submissive male. "Please tell the chef I appreciate the trouble he went to, but unfortunately," she pointed at the plate of dripping steaks. "He only has a taste for that."

"And that is what you shall have." She locked eyes with Galen and found his inner wolf was peeking out at her. "You shall have whatever you need."

I need to leave. I need to save myself. I need to save our child.

"Thank you."

"Anything for you, *agapi mou*." He was touching her again, a wave of tenderness sliding over his features. Tenderness? From him? Sexual heat and burning fury she was familiar with, but she didn't know what to do with this caring. Instead of meeting it, she shied away from his emotions.

Yes, she imagined he would give her anything. Except her freedom. Instead of saying those words aloud, she returned her attention to her place setting, giving the newest server a gratified smile when a hardly seared steak was placed before her. She quickly reached for her silverware, stomach grumbling and growling, anxious for the coming protein. It wasn't until the fork and knife were in her hand that she realized no one else was eating. She shot a look down the table and flicked that same look to Galen.

He answered her unasked question. "The bearing woman eats first and only when she is happy with what is placed before her and begins to eat will the rest of the pack begin."

It was sweet in its own bloody way. She held her silverware tightly, carefully slicing into the butter soft meat and she slowly brought a bite to her lips. The moment it hit her tongue she moaned in appreciation, and even the baby settled with that first nibble. She knew he wouldn't be satisfied by such a small piece but it was the start.

Galen chuckled. "I take it the food is to your satisfaction."

"Yes." He waved to the other servers, but Lissa's entire focus remained on the meal. On cutting away tidbits and feeding herself and her child. This was the first step. The first step in caring for herself and the baby.

43

She would devise a plan, figure out how she could save them both. Or at least save her son.

The meal continued, the soft clink and scrape of silverware on the porcelain plates only interrupted by the occasional laugh and low murmur of voices. Galen was occupied by Andrea's chattering and high-pitched laughter. A spear of jealousy struck her and she fought to push the emotion away. She didn't have a right to be jealous. Hell, she shouldn't even *be* jealous. And yet, even knowing his plans, she wanted him. Some part of her still loved him.

Stupid, stupid girl.

At some point, the others slowly departed, the careful rumble gradually easing until it was her, Galen, and Andrea along with Galen's guards in the room. The other two continued to speak while Lissa ignored them. Or at least tried to. Then again, why bother? It wasn't as if she understood a single word the two exchanged. Sure, she could read body language, but Galen seemed to have only three states. Happy, angry, aroused. At the moment, he was angry and it didn't take much reasoning to figure out why.

Lissa finally nudged her plate away, resting back against the seat and placing her hands atop her belly. The pup was asleep and content, settled in for at least a couple hours before he was demanding food again.

She wasn't sure how she'd cope when he finally came into the world.

Then again, it wouldn't be *her* coping, would it?

The baby trembled, picking up on her unease, and she fought to tear down the emotion. Her doctor in the states constantly reminded her that while human babies could react to a mother's emotions, there was no doubt it occurred with werewolf babies. If she was angry, sad, happy... The baby experienced at all.

Stavros moved from his post and slowly rounded the end of the table, bending close to Galen's left ear. A nearly audible murmured conversation ensued and then Galen focused on her.

"Stavros will return you to your room."

That was it. They'd exchanged a few words in the last two hours and now she was being banished. She fisted one hand, digging her nails into the palm in an effort to suppress her angry words, and the baby responded by tumbling inside her. She took a deep breath to push away the frustration as she rubbed her stomach. The clenching of her fist reminded her of the wounds on her arm that were nearly gone, but she knew blood remained.

Lissa focused on the guard and gave him a small smile. "I would appreciate that, thank you."

She ignored Galen's answering growl and instead was intent on carefully rising from her chair and then making her way down the length of the room. She managed to keep her hands to herself until they exited the large space and entered the hallway. There, she reached out for Stavros, wrapping her fingers around his forearm and using him for support as she made her way to her assigned guestroom. No longer was she housed in the Alpha's suite, which was fine for her. She didn't want to be near him, didn't want to fall in love with him again... Again? She'd never stopped.

She'd never stopped loving him and in the end... it would kill her.

CHAPTER FOUR

THE COOL OCEAN AIR RUFFLED LISSA'S HAIR AND SHE grasped a few errant strands to tuck them behind her ear. She'd taken refuge on the back veranda, Galen and the pack still relaxing inside. The house was filled with wolves on both two feet and four and as a full human, she felt decidedly out of place. The baby stretched and pressed against her stomach, snaring her attention. She placed her palm over a small bulge he caused. She wasn't sure if it was a foot or hand. It was simply her child.

"I'm here for you, sweet pup," she whispered, thankful for the bursts of wind that would wash away her words. "I won't let anything happen to you."

At least not while I'm alive.

She wasn't sure why she tried to hide her thoughts

from the child since he sensed them anyway and squirmed inside her. "Shhh... Give me a break, sweetheart."

The scuffle of feet on the flagstone announced someone's approach. No, not someone—Galen. It was in the way the pup reacted, the way the baby's emotions overrode Lissa's and a timid excitement filled her child. She used to feel the same way when she had Galen in her life. Always on edge, always anxious to be with him, loving every moment they spent together. But that was then.

His warmth bathed her back, his body temperature higher than a normal human's and the heat enveloped her in a soothing embrace. She remembered this about him, remembered that his nearness easily banished any chill in the air. Even the pup seemed at ease with the new heat and calmed in an instant.

"It is cold out, *agapi mou*. Stavros should not have allowed you to venture from the house." Censure was in Galen's voice and Lissa was quick to defend the other wolf.

"It's not as if he could stop me, Galen. He could earn your displeasure by following me outside or his death by touching me. You can't blame the guy for choosing life." She thought she heard Stavros snort, but it quickly transformed into a cough.

"No, apparently I cannot," he drawled and then broke into Greek to issue a quick order and that was followed by Stavros' retreat. "He is gone, but that does not change the fact that you should not be out here."

Lissa shrugged. "I shouldn't *be* here at all."

She'd become used to reading people, sensing emotions that lingered in the air even if she could not scent them like a wolf, and she knew she'd enraged him. "And where should the mother of my child and my child be? On the other side of the ocean? Without my protection?"

This time she snorted and rubbed the now smooth skin on her arms. "Your protection leaves much to be desired."

"You should be thankful Andrea—"

She spun to face him and immediately regretted the decision. She was struck anew by his overwhelming looks, his presence, and the dominance that surrounded him like an ever-present cloak. He wasn't just tall, dark and handsome. He was so much more. He had an animalistic quality that called to something primal within her, that urged her to jump into his arms and disregard their past and embrace the present.

Dangerous.

"Do me a favor. I realize that in your mind I have no

right to ask for anything, but as the mother of your child, I do not want to hear her name pass your lips when we are alone." She wasn't sure what drove her to make the request, but she hoped he granted her that small concession.

A smile teased his lips. "Jealous, *agapi mou*?"

"Hardly." Scared... Furious... Consumed by hatred...

"And what do I get if I agree to this?"

She raised her eyebrows and adopted a hopeful expression. "My undying gratitude?"

He barked out a laugh. "Not quite enough, *agapi mou*."

He traced her face with his gaze, eyes scanning her and not missing a single thing. He skimmed her dark brown hair, the line of her neck, her breasts, which were larger from her pregnancy, and finally the large bulge of her stomach. His face softened, the anger and stress she'd seen on his face since he'd found her now gone, pure love shined from his eyes.

A thought occurred to her and before she could swallow it, it burst from her lips. "How can you look at him inside me, love him so much, and yet hate me?"

He gasped and those eyes that had had been so filled with love were now consumed by anger. Always anger. "I would have to think of you as something more than the mother of my child for you to affect me in any way." His words were harsh and sharp. "You carry my heir. That is all."

Her son's response was instantaneous and it forced her to grasp a nearby pole for support. He was a strong child, a strong werewolf, and his emotions were riotous inside her. But no matter what invaded their lives, a single emotion and response was ever present. Above all he wanted to protect her. Even from within her womb, he battled to keep her from harm and emotional battering.

The low growl vibrated through her, shaking her from inside out and seeming to flow from her pores in a tremulous wave of unending sound. It was soft yet constant, quiet and yet filled with a deadly threat. Her son, so fierce.

Galen stepped forward to grasp her when she'd slumped, but at the reverberating growl, he immediately raised his hands and took a step back. "What the hell is that?"

Lissa focused on soothing the child within her, noting the tenseness of the muscles surrounding her belly. "Your son." She spared not another thought for Galen. "Hush, little one. You remember our visit to Dr. Sanna," she murmured. "Getting upset like this can hurt mama." From what the doctor indicated, a werewolf mother easily handled these types of outbursts, showing her dominance over the baby, but

Lissa was human and thus had more difficulty. He was gradually slowing, the occasional snarl escaping, but the rumble remained. "Hush now." A spear of pain rocked her right side, and she hissed with the piercing ache. "Come on, baby boy." He wasn't letting go. "What did your men bring from my apartment? Any of the prescriptions from my medicine cabinet?"

She hated to take a sedative, but after appearing in the emergency room for the third time from this same complaint, the doctor had given her something safe that would calm the baby.

"No." He frowned and reached for her once again. "We brought a few changes of clothing anything else you needed could be purchased. What is that sound? Why are you growling? What is wrong with you? What is he doing to you?"

"Dammit." She fought for calm. "It's your son. He's very protective. At least give me ten feet of space so I can calm him and keep us both out of the hospital."

For now. At least until the baby felt threatened again.

Galen paled, his normally deep olive skin tone now ghostly white. "Hospital?" He muttered the word as he scrambled backward and then spun on his heel and disappeared into the house.

At least he gave her space.

With his retreat came the ability to breathe and her son immediately relaxed as if knowing that Galen no longer lingered. She released a relieved sigh and carefully waddled toward a nearby chair. With care, she lowered herself to the seat, and worked at steadying her heartbeat.

Unfortunately, she wasn't alone for long. Raised voices burst from the house, growls and snarls interspersed with the rapid shots of Greek and the occasional English word. She did notice that the English words tended to be curses. Without preamble, Galen emerged from the home, his attention scanning the shadows of the veranda, and then he spied her. He stomped toward her, furious intent on his features and the baby started all over again.

"Galen, haven't you done enough? I know I won't live a moment past his birth, but do you think you could let me survive long enough to bring him to term?"

He must have heard something in her tone, the spirit of her words and not just the syllables themselves, because he jerked to a sudden halt and stared at her. His confusion was real and unfeigned. Why was he confused? Because she knew his game? If anything, he should be happy. He wouldn't have to pretend treating her as anything other than the prisoner she was. She didn't need public dinners surrounded by people she didn't know.

Galen turned his head and shouted but didn't step any nearer. Within seconds, a man burst through the double doors and rushed onto the patio. His strides were long and sure, no hints of hesitation or doubt in his brisk movements. The bone structure, the nose and jaw combined with the hair and those eyes, told her she wasn't just looking at another wolf, but a relative of Galen's. The brother. She wondered where Dr. Martin went. Part of her urged her to get away from the man especially when she noted what he carried in his right hand. A black leather bag. One of *those* black leather bags. A staple for all doctors, it seemed.

Lissa shook her head, denying his approach, and grasped the arms of the chair. She trembled, not just from the fear of having a Liakos doctor's hands on her, but also because her pup reacted to his presence as well.

He immediately slid to a stop, hand up, raised in a position of surrender. "Ms. Hill—Melissa—please, calm down."

"I am calm." He had the grace not to call her out on her lie.

"I can hear the pup from here and Galen tells me you are human. If you both can't relax, I'm going to have to sedate you. This isn't healthy for either of you. It could cost you both—"

"—our lives. Yes, I know. I'm trying, but—" she flicked her attention from the doctor to Galen and back again, which prompted the doctor to glance over his shoulder.

He refocused on her, but didn't speak to her. "I need you to leave."

"But—" Galen tried.

"No arguments. You don't get to pull rank on this. For the health of my patient, I want the veranda cleared." He didn't look to see if his request was followed, but then again he was a wolf. He could simply hear everyone's departure.

Yes, everyone left, but Galen lingered in the doorway. At least it gave her breathing room and she could concentrate on her son.

"Can I check you now?"

Already, her son calmed and she nodded. He approached slowly, steps measured and careful, and he gently sat his bag on the ground before dropping to his knees.

"I'm Dr. Perrin Liakos."

"Galen's brother," she murmured.

He nodded. "His brother and also the highest ranking

pack doctor." He flicked open his bag and pulled out a stethoscope. "Mind if I take a listen?"

She shook her head. Why deny him? She wanted her son to be healthy and she needed to accept that for now, she had no control over her situation. She carefully reached for the bottom hem of her shirt to bare her belly to have a snarl freeze her in place. That was followed by one from the doctor and he quickly rose and spun toward the source of the sound.

Galen. Who else?

"You will not expose her to everyone," he snarled at Perrin before turning to her. "You will not expose yourself."

Perrin's voice was calm but firm. "And you will not speak like that to my patient. If you want the mother and child to live, you will begin acting like it or I will admit her. I would take her from the city completely if I could manage it, but I *will* put her in the hospital without hesitation and with full justification if you do not stop behaving this way toward her."

The two men faced off against one another, Perrin standing tall and strong beneath what had to be his Alpha, while Galen seemed just as resolved in his course. The violence was barely suppressed, hovering in the air, and she felt as if anything would set the battle into motion.

"Please." Galen and Perrin remained in place and she wondered if they'd heard her, so she repeated herself. "*Please.*"

Galen released the breath he'd been holding and redirected his attention to her, his fear meeting her eyes for a brief moment before dropping to her stomach and then he was looking elsewhere once again. "I want to know what's wrong with her. I want you to make her well."

Make me well? How about let me go?

"I swear it." Perrin immediately returned.

Galen gave a brisk nod and then spun on his heel and retreated. This time he didn't stop at the doorway but continued deeper into the house and out of sight. No one was within view now, no yellowed eyes of wolves or the brighter hues of humans staring out at her.

Perrin was back, kneeling once again with his stethoscope in hand. "Let's try this again."

Let's not. Instead of putting voice to her words, she merely lifted her shirt up over her belly, and edged the waistband of her pants down to expose the gently undulating mound. With Galen's departure and Perrin's calming presence, the baby was finally relaxing within her.

"Should I have another sonogram?" Worry gnawed at

her. In the past, after each episode, Dr. Sanna had done a sonogram, but she wasn't sure how Perrin handled things.

"Let's just take a listen for now and I'll have a small chat with your son."

Chat?

Then her mental question was answered when Perrin began a low rhythmic song of growls and low rumbles that her son seemed to return in kind. Only a few seconds passed, the exchange seeming to continue, and then the doctor eased back with a smile on his face. "He sounds fine, heartbeat is strong and steady. Are you feeling any pain?"

Lissa took stock of her body, searching for any lingering stinging pain or throbbing aches and found none, so she shook her head and furrowed her brow. "No, and usually I'm sore..."

Perrin nodded. "Yes, that can happen when you're not treated by your pack doctor. A hospital physician doesn't have the connection to the baby like the child's pack doctor would. I'm even further connected to him by our blood bond." He tucked his stethoscope back into his back. "He understands that he hurt you and I'm sure he'll try very hard not to do it again, but pups are sensitive to your emotions."

He didn't have to voice the next order since it was one

she'd heard before. Stay calm. Easier said than done. "So he's fine?"

"You should be worried about yourself, not him. But yes, he's fine."

She released a relieved sigh. "Good. That's... Good. You —you can talk to him? He talked to you?"

He nodded again. "Yes, I have been trained, though 'talk' isn't exactly the right description. He's running on instincts now, but he understands a little better even though we can't use words."

"Wow." She stroked her stomach, amazed at her little boy.

"Yes. I'm always amazed." Perrin opened his mouth to say something and then snapped it closed before finally speaking again. "I know this is my brother's child and I know the two of you have issues." She snorted, but he continued. "But you both need to call a truce for the health of your child. I know more than the pack, but I'm sure there are many things that have been shared between only the two of you. For your sake, for the child's sake, you two need to push it aside and simply make it through this pregnancy." The doctor met her gaze. "You two can hash it out after you give birth, but for now, let the past lie and focus on today and tomorrow."

Their conversation was now leaden and heavy with the

shift and she tried for a light response. "Doctor's orders?"

Rather than smile and chuckle, he simply nodded, a serious expression in place. "Yes. Rest and relaxation. The baby will benefit from having Galen around, so you both need to push your own personal feelings aside and focus on what's best for the child."

Perrin rolled to his feet, now towering above her. He turned away from her, intent on returning to the house, but she had one last question. "Are you saying this because it really is best for my baby and me or because Galen is your brother and you have some misguided sense that we can somehow work things out?"

"You were good together. I'd never seen him so happy before. And then when you left..." He shook his head. "Both. The answer is both."

CHAPTER FIVE

By unspoken agreement, Lissa and Galen followed Perrin's directions to the letter. They had breakfast every morning, Galen murmuring a morning greeting to her before dropping to his knees at her side. The first time he'd done so had been awkward and stilted, but she'd given her permission and accepted his touch. Now it had become commonplace for him to press his ear to her stomach, hands on the roundness as he growled and "spoke" to their son. They still refrained from conversing more than necessary, but they weren't together because they were in a relationship, it was for their son.

She simply had to remind her heart of that daily.

Such as when he took her for walks through the expansive gardens or when he paced at her side while they toured some of the small shops and prepared the nursery. Those were the most difficult times, when she would stare at an adorable blanket or an even cuter stuffed animal and know that while it might bring a smile to her child, she would never see it. Yet each time those thoughts stirred, her pup responded in kind which drew Galen's attention.

Those thoughts encroached as she rested in a window seat, attention on the young werewolves frolicking in the yard. Some were toddlers, some teens, but their joy was unmistakable no matter the age.

What will you look like when you're that age?

As if her thoughts and unease had drawn him, Galen stepped into the room. He was six feet of pure male and unquestioned dominance. He was dressed in one of his typical suits yet he'd abandoned the jacket, tie, and even his shoes before he sought her out. It was something she'd recognized early on. If he could remove his shoes, he would. Always.

"*Agapi mou*?" He met her gaze and then his attention dropped to her stomach, to the rolling wave that trembled through her flesh.

"I'm fine. How was your day?" Trivialities and small talk. It seemed that's all they were good for nowadays.

He frowned and ignored her question as he padded toward her. He lowered himself and knelt at her side, his lips immediately pressing against her undulating stomach and his hands stroking her roundness. Familiar rumbles poured over her, the sounds soothing and comforting in their rhythm and tone. She closed her eyes and leaned back against the wall, relaxing.

She hadn't even realized he'd stopped until he spoke. "What has you upset?"

Lissa shook her head. "Nothing."

That single word had become their code word for the past and when she used it, he frowned even harder. He remained silent for a moment, his eyes seeming to will her to tell him more, but she remained mute on the issue. Perrin had been clear. She shouldn't get upset, should shy away from what caused her distress. Now wasn't the time.

But Perrin doesn't know that there never will be a time.

"Then let us give you something." He easily rolled to his feet and held a hand out for her. "Come. I have a surprise that will please you both."

The teasing smile that graced his lips reminded her of the Galen she'd met all those months ago. The one who had quick grins and a passion that seemed unending.

Passion. That word kindled thoughts of his mouth on hers, his hands tracing her curves and his lips following that same path. He'd been her first. Her only. And he'd showed her what could truly be between a man and a woman. Showed her how a wolf loved a female and put his brand on her, on her heart and soul. Now, so close to delivery, her body was warming and aching for him. One smile and that's all it took. There had to be something *wrong* with her. How could she be this attracted to a man who was so quick to destroy her?

When those brown eyes sparkled and slowly slipped to yellow, she had her answer. He was everything to her, two halves of a whole and all she'd ever desired in one male.

That smile slowly heated and his nostrils flared and she knew he scented her burgeoning desire.

Unacceptable. The last thing she wanted was for him to realize she still craved him.

"Great." She placed her hand on his and carefully slid from the window seat. Her growing stomach made rising difficult, but Galen was quick to assist her. "Lead the way."

The small smirk teasing his lips told her he was on to her game of avoidance. Instead of replying, he led her toward the archway, only pausing when Leo turned the corner and came into view. She noticed he carried a pair of sturdy sandals with thick, gripping soles. Similar to those Galen bought her when she first came to his home. Ones that made the descent to the beach safer.

The beach...

"You're taking me..."

Leo arrived, handing over the small burden and Galen dropped into a crouch and reached for one of her bare feet. "Down to the beach? Yes."

"But you said it was too dangerous."

Galen met her gaze through his thick lashes. "As Perrin likes to point out, I am occasionally overbearing and wrong."

Leo twitched and Lissa didn't miss the tightening of the other man's jaw and the tenseness and anger that seemed to consume the other wolf at those words.

"But—"

He slid the last strap into place and then pushed to his feet once again, reaching for her in that same move. "But nothing. We will take the steps slowly and you will listen to me."

Excitement bubbled within her, and not even his autocratic words could diminish the feelings. "Yes, yes." She would have bounced on her toes like a child if she was sure she wouldn't topple over. "From the moment I put my foot on the first step to the last, I swear."

"And all of those before and after, as well," he countered.

There was a teasing glint in his eyes and some of her old feelings of closeness and caring resurfaced. "I'm not so sure about that, but I'm open to negotiation."

That was a joke they'd often shared, the fast and furious negotiations Galen enjoyed in the boardroom then brought into the bedroom on a softer much more sensual scale. When he licked his lips, exposing his sharpened white fangs, she knew his mind went there as well.

"We'll see." He reached for her hand and she readily welcomed his touch. "Let's get you down there first."

Lissa wasn't worried. While she admitted to being a little more unbalanced than usual, she was still very agile and quick on her feet. She had to be considering her profession before Galen found her. So while he spent fifteen minutes growling during a trip that used to take only five minutes, she focused on the ocean, the crashing waves, and the clean scent of the sea.

The pups that had been playing in the yard now peeked over the edge of the cliff, watching their careful trudge down the steps. She kept glancing up at them, noticing the sad kicked puppy expressions they each had.

"Watch where you're going!" His roar was swallowed by the ocean, as was her sigh of annoyance.

Lissa paused and looked over her shoulder at him. "I am watching. I'm fine. I just thought that it was sad that my presence means the pups can't play on the beach." She gestured toward the small gathering. "Look at them."

Galen sighed. "You're going to be a pushover for our son, aren't you?"

A spear of sadness, a bolt of emotional pain she didn't want to experience, struck her and she was quick to shove it back into the hole it crawled out of. Now was not the time. The stairs was not the place. So she adopted a smile and upbeat tone and hoped he didn't try and look deeper. "I seem to be a sucker for a good-looking man."

He gave her a skeptical look, as if he didn't believe her in the slightest but remained silent. "Uh-huh. The pups are down here nearly every day. They can wait a few hours. Besides, everyone knows we cater to a bearing woman." He slowly eased closer and placed his hand on her stomach. It was the first time he'd touched her for something other than speaking to their son. It was the first he'd initiated since they were reunited. "They carry the future of the pack."

Right. She almost forgot she was merely the incubator. Instead of saying another word, Lissa nodded and returned to her path, carefully picking her way down the steps. It seemed to take forever, but eventually her sandaled feet were standing on soft sand and the ocean spread out before her in a large blanket of blue.

"It's gorgeous," she whispered.

"Yes," his voice was just as soft and she realized that instead of looking at their scenery surrounding them, he was staring at her.

Their gazes connected, eyes locked upon each other, and it was as if the recent weeks and dreadful months melted away. It was like the first day he'd ever drawn her down to the sandy shore and shown her this small slice of his personal heaven.

It was a place she savored but didn't want to return to. There was no joy or answers to be found there.

Swallowing hard and clearing her throat, she shuffled away and grasped the roughhewn stone cliff face. She reached for her ankle, raising her leg at the same time, and realized it so wasn't happening. She tried again, straightening and then bending downward in an attempt to grab her ankle, and yet again was unsuccessful. A little chuckle came from her left and she shot him a glare before trying the third time.

"*Agapi mou*, there is a reason I placed the shoes on your feet." He strolled forward and lowered himself, reaching for her ankle and carefully cradling her foot. "Because it means that I can remove them—something —from you."

And wasn't that more than a little suggestive?

"You don't want to take anything off me. You hate me," she blurted out the words before she could think better of them. It was the truth whether she wanted to say the words aloud or not.

Galen didn't say anything, merely continued unbuckling her shoes and carefully lowering her bare feet to the pale sand. When he was done, he easily stood, her shoes gathered in one hand and he reached for her with the other. He twined their fingers together as if they were lovers and led her toward the water. As they neared the rolling waves, she noticed the large umbrella, blankets, and basket off to their left.

A picnic. It was... sweet. Sweet and hinted at a caring she knew he couldn't feel toward her.

He dropped her shoes near the pile and then they continued toward the gentle waves. They moved forward as one until the cool water tickled her toes and then they merely stopped and stared out at the ever-reaching ocean before them. Some nights they would do this, silently stand at the water's edge and enjoy the deepening sunset. The only difference between then and now was that only their fingers touched when, in the past, they used to be wrapped around each other.

The water splashed her ankles, chilling her, and she let the rhythmic waves soothe her just as she took comfort from the feel of his hand in hers. She wasn't sure how long they quietly remained in place, but it was Galen who broke the silence.

"I don't hate you." She opened her eyes and focused on him, unable to believe his words. "I hate what you did, I don't understand it, but I don't hate *you*." He sighed. "And I don't know what to do any longer," he growled. "Perrin will not allow us to talk about the past, but I cannot let go of it if I cannot talk to you about it, but to rehash, could threaten my future."

She had no doubt about what "future" he referenced. Especially when his stare dropped to her stomach. That "future" definitely didn't include her.

"I know you want to hash things out, but I'm not sure why. What would talking about it change? When he's born, you're going to do exactly what you plan on doing, my wishes and hopes be damned." He opened his mouth as if to speak and she pushed on. "No. The 'why' no longer matters."

"Maybe not to you—"

"Of course it concerns me. But as soon as he's born you get what you want. What good is talking about this when the result is the same?" She looked out over the waves, enjoying the waning heat of the sun as it set and cast colors into the sky. "Let me enjoy this, Galen." She returned her attention to him. "Let me enjoy my pregnancy, let me enjoy carrying him, and let later take care of itself."

He stroked her with his stare, those eyes scanning her face. She knew what he saw, the shadowed lines of fatigue and worry as well as the dark bags under her eyes. Despite her words and desire to live in the present, the past still dogged her sleep.

He stepped closer and she didn't have the good sense to back away. Not when a familiar tenderness filled his gaze immediately followed by a small frown. His hands rose, palms coming to rest on her cheeks. "I have been pushing you and that is unforgivable." He leaned forward and pressed his lips to her for head, speaking against her skin. "No more. I swear it. We will bring this pup into the world with happy parents."

Damn him for teasing her, for tormenting her, but she refused to reveal her knowledge, hoping he'd see his error before it was too late. "Okay."

"Excellent." He released her face and snared her left

hand, entwining their fingers and then carefully leading her deeper into the water. "Come. I know you love the waves and this will make our pup happy."

He wasn't lying on either count. Their baby was unmistakably excited and enjoying her happiness in the ocean. For now, she would push everything away. No future. No past. There was only now with Galen. With his wide smile, sparkling eyes, and glorious body.

When had he discarded his shirt? Because now he was bare from the waist up, his muscles bulging and stretching his skin, taunting her with his deliciously carved form. Her mouth watered, memories of tasting every inch of him as he taught her the joys of lovemaking. He loved it when she bit him, when she sank her teeth into his flesh just short of piercing his skin. And it didn't matter where. His chest, his shoulder, even his inner thigh though those nearby bits were totally off-limits.

Her body immediately responded to his unclothed state, her nipples pebbling and heat settling between her thighs. No matter what, she craved him. Craved him more than any other and she imagined she always would.

She shivered, desire unfurling and gently sliding through her. He narrowed his eyes the tiniest bit and then the color flashed yellow for the barest of moments before his inner wolf was banished again. It was obvious the wolf wanted her, but she figured that was instinctual. She carried Galen's pup. It made sense.

"Are you cold?"

So he was trying to pretend he didn't know why she trembled. "No." She shook her head. "I'm fine, I don't want to miss this."

A larger wave splashed against her thighs, and she took an involuntary step back. In that instant, Galen was there. His front plastered to her back, arms sliding around her waist and settling on the curve of her stomach.

"Careful."

Careful? Careful about what? She couldn't think of anything besides the overwhelming warmth that struck her with his closeness. Not just the heat, but also the knowledge that his bare skin was so close. And then there was *his* body's reaction to *her*. His hardness was unmistakable, his length firmly pressing into her back.

"I—" she cleared her throat. "I'm fine."

He hummed and lowered his head, lips brushing the shell of her ear. "Then humor me, *agapi mou*, and allow me this."

It was almost as if he asked permission, but she knew that was insane. An alpha never asked for anything. He merely assumed that whatever he desired was his due. When she didn't reply, he nuzzled her, the rough hair on his cheeks scraping her pale skin and sending a tremble of the need down her spine.

"*Agapi mou*?"

Was that the scrape of his fangs over her skin? It was something he used to do, teeth scratching her neck and shoulders, and she'd always loved it. Still loved it.

Perrin wanted them to live in the now? Then she would.

"Of course." She leaned back against him, reveling in this closeness.

Her hips and ass brushed his firm length and she didn't shy from his hardness, but embraced it. Did she know their plans? Know what was to come? Yes. But while they had their ideas, she had her own.

Ones about trying to escape once again. But first... First she'd enjoy this cease fire and take whatever Galen was willing to give and pray those memories would carry her through the tough times ahead. Because it seemed she *could* love and hate him at the same time.

"Melissa? What are you doing? What are you offering?"

She carefully turned sideways, continuing to allow him

to support her, and tilted her head back. "That depends on you. On whether you meant…"

He ran his fingers down her face, tracing the line of her jaw and then brushing the tips over her lips. His eyes were focused on that part of her and she could practically read his thoughts. He'd taught her how to do so many things with her mouth. Kiss. Taste. *Suck.*

"I want you. I will not deny this. But I will not risk our child."

Lissa shook her head, falling a little more in love with him. She knew his sex drive. Knew how much wolves needed that release, which reminded her of how much time they spent apart. Had he gone to Andrea?

It didn't matter. Lissa was here now. At least, she pretended it didn't matter as she hid from the truth.

She took too long to reply, hesitated and then no longer had the chance to tell him that Perrin told her that making love with Galen was safe.

Galen lowered his head and captured her lips in a passionate and punishing kiss. It was a violent meeting of mouths, his tongue delving into her, tasting her, and she returned the favor. She moaned with the first burst of his flavors over her taste buds. She'd missed this. Missed his smoky and sweet taste. Missed the way his sharpened fangs scraped her lower lip without breaking the delicate skin.

He nibbled and sucked, teased and tormented, and all the while growls rumbled in his chest. The longer the kiss continued, the more dominant he became until one hand was buried in her hair and he used that grip to move her head as he desired. He tilted her ever so slightly, taking their kiss even deeper, and she discovered that the ultimate release was nearly upon her from his small attentions alone. She ached and throbbed for him, desperate to have him inside her, to become one with him.

She whimpered and leaned against him, allowing him to take her full weight. It was that subtle shift, that transference of weight that ended in their kiss. He tore his mouth from hers, continuing to support her while he turned his head away. His chest heaved with heavy pants and Lissa discovered she was having just as much trouble breathing. Arousal and need for him thrummed in her veins, and she bit back the urge to beg him for more.

Slowly her heart rate returned to normal, easing until she was able to breathe clearly once again. Galen took one last deep breath and released it slowly before returning his attention to her.

"That... was a mistake."

It felt as if he'd punched her in the chest, crushing her heart as he broke her bones. "Oh." She wasn't sure how she got the single syllable past her lips, but she did. "I see."

Then he was touching her again, sliding his arms around her increased bulk. "It is simply a mistake to start something I cannot finish." He dropped his gaze to her mouth. "I always told you your mouth was dangerous and you know I cannot stop with just a kiss. Not with you. I never could." His lips twisted in a small grimace. "And that is something of the past."

At least this time that single thought didn't bring rage to his features.

"Come. It is late and soon the sun will be gone. Today is not the day for a picnic. Let me lead you inside where it is safe."

Safe. Right.

CHAPTER SIX

LISSA WASN'T SURE HOW HE'D MANAGED IT, BUT A WEEK later, she stepped out of the bathroom after a long hot shower to find a gorgeous evening gown laid out on the bed. It was a deep teal, the sumptuous fabric like silk to the touch and it was so light, it almost felt like air. The cut was beautiful, clinging yet not, flowing yet not. She wouldn't look like she was wearing a circus tent, but she also wouldn't look like a stuffed sausage.

"It will look beautiful on you." The deep masculine voice sent a shiver of need down her spine.

She held the massive bath sheet in place and turned toward Galen. He leaned negligently against the doorway, arms crossed over his chest and ankles crossed as well. His hair was windblown and unruly, his pristine white shirt was wrinkled, the top few buttons undone and the arms were rolled up and pushed to his elbows which exposed his deeply tanned and strong forearms. His slacks were equally disheveled, the harsh straight creases now flattened while other wrinkles took up residence along his legs. And... he was barefoot.

"You look..." Like he'd just rolled out of bed. How many times had he had this rumpled look after they'd spent an afternoon together? They'd tease and torment each other as they went about their day, race up the stairs, clinging and ripping at each other's clothing and leaving them wherever they lay. Later he'd slide into them once again so he could hunt up food for them. This. This was exactly what she used to see.

Whose bed did he just leave?

She didn't have the right to ask.

Galen gave her a small smile. "Exhausted."

From what?

"This merger is exhausting me from sunup to sundown."

Merger. She hadn't heard it called that before.

"If you're too tired to go out..." She let her statement drift away, waiting for him to fill in the blanks.

Galen shook his head. "No. I've been looking forward

to this all day. I saw this dress and thought of you. I can't wait to see you in it."

The heat that filled his gaze told her he couldn't wait to see her out of it, either. Was he that insatiable? Looking as if he'd just climbed from one woman's bed and he was anxious to find his way into hers?

The true question was—did she care?

No.

She was savoring the present, reveling in today and not worrying about yesterday or tomorrow.

"Oh. Okay."

He pushed away from the doorway and slowly padded toward her, his footsteps silent. When he reached for her, she gladly went into his arms and enjoyed the feel of his arms holding her closely. He brought his mouth to hers, lips brushing over her flesh in a soft caress that began chaste and slowly deepened to more. He gently slipped his tongue into her mouth and she welcomed him, sinking into his kiss with complete abandon. This was as far as they'd gone since that moment in the ocean, their connections limited to their mouths no matter how much she ached to stroke him.

But... That could be at an end. She'd spoken with Perrin earlier in the day...

He carefully lifted his head and eased back but didn't release her. "I've been looking forward to that all day."

"So have I."

He hummed. "Leo tells me Perrin was here to see you. That he stayed for quite a while and pulled rank on Leo, kicking him from the room." She could practically see the jealousy and anger roaring inside Galen's mind, the shutters sliding down over his eyes as it slowly consumed him. "What was so important to say that he would be dismissed? What is going on between you and my brother?"

Lissa shook her head. "Nothing. I had an appointment with my doctor and he said all is well."

Along with a few other things.

Galen immediately released her and took a large step back. "I will not be cuckolded in my own home. You are mine. You will never be alone with another male again. I forbid it."

Lissa furrowed her brow. "Galen..." She shook her head. "We—"

"Hear me on this. I will tell him the same."

"He's my doctor. He came to see me about the baby."

A low growl tumbled from his lips. "Hear me."

"Galen—"

He took a deep breath and moved farther away from her, going to the door. "Get dressed. We're leaving in an hour."

With that, he spun and left, disappearing down the hallway and leaving her standing in the middle of her room wearing nothing but a towel and a mixture of anger and bewilderment on her face.

"What the hell just happened?" she murmured to herself.

Whatever just occurred, it was going to be hashed out over dinner. Her stomach growled for food—or was that the baby—and the gorgeous dress called to her.

She padded to the door, and pushed it closed on silent hinges before returning to her preparations for the evening. She was thankful she'd never gotten into heavy makeup and intricate hairstyles as well as the fact that Galen's men hadn't dragged all the makeup she owned across the Atlantic. That meant that getting ready was a matter of blow-drying her hair, putting a little gloss on her lips and a hint of color on her cheeks as well as a dash of mascara. All things she'd snared on their first trip to town together.

The dress was easy to slip into, the designer seeming to realize that dressing was an intricate and interesting dance for pregnant women.

She was ready to go a good fifteen minutes prior to

Galen's stated time and she donned the beautiful flats he'd also given her that matched the dress. Ever so carefully she made her way downstairs and to the formal salon. The room was empty and quiet since no one typically used the space and she slowly made her way toward the massive window that overlooked the main driveway and the glittering city below.

As much as she despised Galen for his plans, she couldn't fault the man for what he would be able to give their son. All the advantages of his money and position would be nothing but a benefit to their child. Especially since he would have Andrea as his mother.

The thought brought a heavy sadness to her heart and stinging tears to her eyes. She needed to discuss it with Galen, see if she could get him to change his mind.

Something drew her attention, some low sound or disturbance in the air, and she tore her attention from the scenery and to the room's entry.

Andrea.

The woman was beautiful as always, her lithe body, gentle curves, and striking features always drew the eyes of men. With the clinging dress now hugging her form, she was both gorgeous and sexy. She had no doubt more than one wolf chased after her tail.

Galen as well?

"Melissa," the sweet tone was there even as the woman's face turned into an evil sneer. "How lovely to see you."

"And you." She knew Andrea could scent her lie but didn't give a damn.

"Going out for the evening?"

"As you can see."

Andrea strolled the deeper into the room, her hips swaying from side to side with pure feminine confidence. "Surprising. I didn't believe Galen had any energy left in him after our day together."

The use of his name, his appearance when he'd returned home combined with the suggestion he had been with Andrea all day, pierced her heart. It was naïve of her to believe he wouldn't visit another woman's bed. He anticipated raising their son with Andrea—the woman was the Alpha bitch—so of course they would be intimate.

"Unless he has changed over the months we were apart, he has quite a bit of stamina and endurance. I don't have to tell you that he can be insatiable, do I?"

With Lissa's reminder, Andrea's eyes flashed and her fangs dropped to prick the woman's lower lip. Perhaps Lissa was wrong. Perhaps...

Andrea took a deep breath and rolled her shoulders

and Lissa watched as the woman's wolf retreated. She licked her lips, gathering the droplets of blood, and the small wounds healed before Lissa's eyes. "Of course you don't. His stamina is something I know well." She tilted her head to the side, as if listening for something and then delivered one last parting shot. "Enjoy your dinner for I will be enjoying *your* dessert."

Lissa heard the sharp click of men's shoes on the marble of the foyer and in less than a second, Galen was framed in the doorway looking his impeccable self once again.

"Alpha," Andrea purred. "I see you have recovered after our long and hard day. I'm so gratified to see that. Perhaps after your dinner," she paused and flashed another one of those sneers her way. "I can *speak* with you again."

Bitch.

"Of course," he quickly responded, his gaze traveling up and down Andrea's body, and the knife in her heart twisted.

Gritting her teeth, she stepped forward and drew his attention back to her. "Galen? Do we have reservations to keep?"

She'd been trying to forget the past. She truly had. But this—his visit to Andrea's bed while raining kisses on Lissa—blew those plans sky high. She would say her piece and then leave all of this behind. She'd been lulled into complacency over the past few weeks, but that was gone.

Galen's head snapped back and he swung his attention to her as if he'd forgotten she was in the room. "What? Yes. Yes, we have reservations." He looked to Andrea. "I will come to you when I return."

When you return alone.

Now it was Andrea's turn to face her, that victorious smile now splitting her lips. "Wonderful, I can't wait."

Lissa didn't say another word as she strode toward the couple, nor did she speak when she strode past them and to the massive front door. Both Stavros and Leo stood nearby, but it was Stavros who leapt into action and quickly opened the door for her as Leo merely glared at her. But when that glare banished in an instant, she knew that Galen was right behind her.

Stavros abandoned the door when he saw Leo would not assist Lissa down the stairs, and he presented his arm for her use, elbow raised arm bent so she could grip him as she descended. A growl followed them, but the man at her side didn't hesitate in his assistance and merely kept pace with her as she continued to the driveway.

The rush of steps indicated Galen's rapid approach, and he finally met her at the door to their limo just as

Stavros was aiding her into the vehicle. Another growl had the guard carefully retreating, and she realized the male was not cowering beneath Galen's anger.

"You do not touch her," Galen snarled.

Stavros merely shrugged but remained silent, his attention flicking to her, his gaze encompassing her in one glance before returning to his Alpha. "You would have me not treat her as she deserves? Your attention was *engaged* elsewhere. Our pack has always put bearing women above all others. Is that not so?"

As polite put down went, it was effective. Galen's cheeks reddened for a brief moment before anger rushed forward again. "No one touches her."

"As you say, Alpha." Stavros tilted his head to the side, but not in the full submission. Even Lissa recognized that.

What had changed? Why was this male who often remained silent about Lissa's treatment suddenly taking his Alpha to task?

Galen crawled into the back with her, anger still present on his features, and the moment the door closed, he also put up the partition between the guards and them. "Do not ever do that again. I needed to speak with Andrea." When he said her name, Lissa tried to remain calm, she truly did. "And your childish behavior nearly cost a wolf his life. No one touches you and I will kill anyone who dares."

"My behavior?" She gasped and grasped the door handle when the limo lurched into motion. She wasn't going to address his threat. He wouldn't kill someone over touching her. That had to be an exaggeration. "Childish? You're joking, right?"

"No. I don't not understand your jealousy and dislike of Andrea. She has been my Alpha bitch for years and I leaned heavily on her during your disappearance. You should appreciate the sacrifices she made on your behalf." He snarled at her, but she latched on to the word sacrifices.

"Sacrifices? *Sacrifices.*" She turned in her seat to stare at him. "Are you kidding? You think that she's done anything out of the kindness of her heart? No, it was to further your plans. Don't put this on me. Don't pretend that she's sweetness and light while you two are scheming behind my back."

"What are you talking about? What is wrong with you?" he growled.

"Me?" She realized she was asking a lot of questions and not getting answers. "I'm—" She bit off the rest of her words and took a deep breath. "I'm not discussing this. I asked you not to say her name or speak about her in my presence."

"Your jealousy is tiresome." Fire filled his eyes.

"Your idiocy is tiresome," she countered.

"Melissa..." There was no missing the warning in his tone.

"What?" She curled her lip and an invitation of a wolf warning.

"Andrea is—"

She lifted her hand, palm out to silence him. "I *will not* do this."

The car rolled to a stop, and she immediately reached for the handle, intent on escaping the vehicle. She managed to yank at the handle and get the door open before Galen stopped her. Hell, she'd even managed to place her feet on the asphalt and half rise from her seat. He snared a bundle of fabric which effectively halted her in her tracks.

"Andrea is of my pack and will always be a part of my pack. Lose the jealousy. It is no longer amusing."

Lissa fought for calm and met his gaze with an unwavering stare. "Hatred and jealousy are not the same thing. So while you're fucking your mistress beside our baby's crib, remember you have to sleep at some point. And if I'm dead by then, I will haunt you until you die. Tell me, is that amusing?"

CHAPTER SEVEN

Lissa flashed the maître d' a smile of thanks as he carefully assisted her into her seat, the man practically tripping over himself to give her whatever she desired.

Galen. You can give me Galen.

However, it seemed no one could, because he was still tied to Andrea. The moment they'd stepped into the restaurant, his cell phone rang and Lissa got a quick peek at the caller ID. Surprise, surprise. Andrea.

"Thank you, so much. A glass of water would be wonderful. We'll order once Galen completes his call."

"Galen has finished his call." He inserted smoothly as he glided forward. "Thank you for assisting my mate."

"Of course, Alpha." The male stepped back and a waiter took his place.

"Good evening, my name is Alfredo and tonight the chef has prepared…" Lissa got lost amongst the dishes recited to her, the different preparations and meals twining together and getting twisted in her mind until by the time the male fell silent, she was simply aching for food. She didn't care what.

"They will not order from the menu. I am making just the thing for the Alpha and his lovely lady, Andrea. I did not get to prepare this for them last night. Shoo-shoo…"

His lovely lady Andrea. Once again she was reminded that she shouldn't allow her hopes to grow simply because it was so painful when they were dashed. She locked eyes with Galen and she had no doubt he saw the pain that filled her expression. At least he didn't bother with placating apologies. Instead, she merely got a rueful grin. In that moment, her future became startlingly clear. Alone or with the help of another, she was leaving. She'd almost allowed herself to believe she could talk to Galen about what she'd overheard, about what Andrea had told her, but why?

A large, barrel chested man came hurrying around the corner. "Alpha, I scented you all the way in the kitchen. You and your lady will—" The man stumbled to a stop. "Oh."

"Quite." Galen quipped. He went through the introductions, giving her information about the restaurant's chef and Galen's history with the man, but Lissa couldn't have cared less. Her only thoughts centered on how often did he flipped between her and Andrea?

It didn't matter. She needed to stop torturing herself. If this wasn't further proof of why she needed to find a way to escape, she wasn't sure what else was needed.

She must have murmured some sort of polite greeting, because it wasn't long before the waiter and the chef drifted away, leaving Lissa and Galen alone in the secluded alcove.

"It is not as it seems. Many in the pack believed—"

"It doesn't matter." She lifted the napkin from her lap and carefully placed it on the table top. "Do you know where I can find the ladies room?"

A worried frown increased his brow. "Is anything wrong?"

"No. I simply need the facilities." *And a moment to compose myself.*

He lifted his hand in a casual way, and the waiter rushed forward. A murmured conversation and then the male was gone as Galen rose from his seat. "Come, I will take you."

She shook her head. "No. Just direct to me."

"Melissa, this is not the time to—"

"Why?" she hissed. "Afraid I'll embarrass the big bad Alpha?" She pushed to her feet and ignored his outstretched hand. "I think you're doing that quite well yourself. How does the pack feel about you fucking your Alpha bitch while I'm pregnant with your pup?" She snorted. "That's right, they're probably in on the plan, too." She stepped closer, sneer in place and all attempts at being discreet gone. "All of this talk, all of these assurances that you don't want to hurt me or our child. Let me tell you something, *Alpha*, if you take my baby, that will kill me. Do you consider that harm?"

"I don't know what you're talking about, but this is not the place." The words were low and growled, the sounds silencing everyone else in the restaurant.

"You're right. This isn't the place for argument and this isn't the place for me. I know your plans and I refuse to go along with them. I thought you were coming to care —" She snapped off the rest of her sentence. "But you're playing us both aren't you? Or am I just being played while you two fuck yourselves through a day and then laugh about the pregnant woman who you seduced, impregnated and then you're going to steal her child while *disposing* of her?" She shook her head. "It doesn't matter. I'm done. You want to keep me captive? Kill me? Tell that to your whole fucking pack. Half of them are here, aren't they? Tell them what kind of leader they have. What kind of Alpha bitch rules at his side? *Tell them!*"

Her human roar rang through the air, hanging over them all and she could feel the stare of every person in the space. Every *wolf* in the space. She had no doubt they all had the ability to drop to four feet and transform into beasts.

And now they knew. Or at least had the truth put to words by Lissa.

Galen snared her bicep, grip firm but still gentle as he turned her toward the front of the restaurant. He lowered his voice but still spoke loudly enough for her to hear. That meant everyone else could as well with their enhanced ability. "I don't know what's got into you. Is this some sort of hormone thing? Perrin warned me—"

Perrin warned Lissa about a lot of things too. Specifically the fact that she needed to remain calm, needed to keep from getting over excited because when she did...

When she did, her son reacted. The first wave of pain hit her when they were half way to the entry, the roll of her son inside her sending a bolt of agony down her spine. She stumbled and caught herself on a nearby chair. The only thing that kept it from toppling was the fact it held an occupant. The sudden move had her out of Galen's hold and so she now clutched her stomach with that free hand. She gasped and heaved, fighting for air and battling to banish the agony.

"Melissa!"

She ignored him, but she couldn't ignore his hands on her. Not when their son reacted to the connection by stretching and growling. It was too soon. She couldn't give birth yet, but he didn't want to listen.

"What is wrong with you?"

"You." She snapped and the baby seemed intent on clawing his way out of her to attack Galen.

Shouts and snarls of Greek filled the air, one voice on top of another, and she tuned them out as she focused on her baby. Large calloused hands grasped her and she gasped, shooting her gaze to the owner. She marginally relaxed when she met Stavros his gaze.

"Come. I take you home now. Perrin is meeting us there."

Lissa shook her head. She didn't want to go there ever again.

"Yes. Yes. I know my Alpha and what you are saying cannot be true. It hurts the baby, yes? Perrin will assist you and I will keep the baby safe."

"No." She shook her head, but then he didn't give her a

choice. With Stavros' touch and Galen's distance, her son calmed and the large male easily swept her into his arms. A wide path opened to them, and then they were striding toward the front entrance and through the doors.

Leo stood there, his dislike still present and palpable, but seeming to be slightly less harsh. Why? Did he finally realized his Alpha wasn't the wonderful man all assumed him to be?

It didn't matter. The pack didn't matter. None of this mattered. She was done being a pushover. A good bit of the pack filled the restaurant tonight and by morning, everyone would know how Galen was treating her and his plans. She imagined he'd be happy to see the back of her come morning.

Stavros carefully slid her into the back of the limo and joined her, issuing orders to Leo in a spattering of Greek and then they were on their way. She closed her eyes, the throbbing pain from her son now settling into a low pulsing ache. She closed her eyes as they navigated the streets, unwilling to watch the scenery speed by. She knew enough to understand that Leo had called Perrin and that they were headed to Galen's villa while he handled the problem she'd created.

She'd created? No. It was him. Him and that Alpha bitch.

It seemed like she just closed her eyes and then she was opening them again as the limo pulled to a stop. Once again she was carried and Stavros did not stop moving until they'd reached her room. Perrin was already there waiting for her. He brought his portable ultrasound along with other testing devices and had already pulled back the covers for her.

"Perrin..."

"No talking. Get changed and get into bed." He was issuing orders as only a doctor could.

Stavros lowered her to her feet and finally slipped his arms from around her but spoke to Perrin. "The Alpha ordered the house cleared of all but the necessary staff. Leo is outside the door. Call out if you need anything."

Leo. He'd just as soon leave her to rot than help her.

"Let's see what you've done to yourself." Perrin reached for her and she scooted away.

"I'm tired of hearing that. I've done nothing but get pregnant by your piece of shit brother. Everything is my fault. Everything that happens is due to something I've done. I'm just..." She hated that tears stung her eyes.

"Okay... Shhh... It's a joke, Melissa. Breathe with me now. You know this isn't good for either of you."

"Galen isn't good for either of us."

"I know, and he won't come near you without your permission. I thought..." He shook his head. "I didn't realize what was between you two, but now..." He held out his hand, palm up. "Let me help you."

Her baby whimpered. She *felt* him whimper, and that made the choice for her. She padded to the doctor and allowed him to help her, allowed him to ease her to the bed and then assist her in retaining her balance as she changed and he kept his gaze averted through it all.

Before long, she was resting on the mattress as Perrin examined her and subsequently the baby via ultrasound. It didn't take him long to confirm that her son was fine and Lissa hadn't been injured. When he was done, he packed away his tools and stood to leave. He moved toward the end of the bed and stopped to glance over his shoulder at her.

"Leo told me what you said and—" she opened her mouth to stop his attempts at justifying his Alpha's behavior. "Just wait. I'm not saying you're unjustified or mistaken in your beliefs. I don't know what's going on between you two or what made you think what you do, but the last thing he would ever do is harm you physically or keep you away from the baby. He hates even letting you out of his sight. You're his *mate*. This distance between you is slowly killing him."

She grimaced. "I'm sure. That's why he's turning to Andrea. Pulled the other leg."

Perrin shook his head and faced her once again, arms crossed over his chest. "He couldn't betray you even if that was the one thing he desired above all other. You're his *mate*."

"I don't know what that means."

Shock filled his features. "Melissa, you're it for him. Wolves mate for life, and you're his. You're pregnant with his pup."

She rolled her eyes, unable to believe his words. "Accidental pregnancies happen all the time."

He shook his head. "Not for wolves. The fact you conceived his child proves your claim on him. Our people are able to conceive children via in vitro if necessary, but natural pregnancy only occurs between mates."

And there's nothing more natural than what we did together.

Perrin continued. "Each wolf has one mate, and you're his."

"I wish I could believe you." *I wish I could believe that Andrea is lying.*

"Try. For you, for the child, for the pack. Just try." He sighed. "Galen is keeping away from the villa and it'll be just you and his most trusted guards tonight. We'll see how you feel in the morning and then I think you two need to talk."

"I would—"

"As your doctor and as a member of the Liakos pack, I'm asking you to talk to my brother, my Alpha. If you need someone nearby, I'll be here, but after the restaurant... things are in turmoil. We need you two to work things out in some way so he can restore order to the wolves. Right now," he shook his head. "It's not looking good."

Her heart froze. "What do you mean?"

"A wolf being accused of abusing his mate is a very serious thing and what you said in the restaurant is being repeated to one and all. There are rumblings of removing Galen."

She shook her head. "I don't know what that means."

"The only way an alpha can be removed is through challenge... and death."

CHAPTER EIGHT

THE NEXT MORNING, LISSA PULLED ON A PAIR OF LOOSE fitting pants and a clinging maternity top. Both outlined the large bulge of her stomach and were easy to move aside for Perrin's examination. Now all she had to do was wait for him. Leo had already brought her a breakfast tray filled with meat which she'd eaten without hesitation and now she rested on a window seat, staring out at the riotous ocean. The waves were much like how she felt. Tumultuous and uneasy, unable to settle. Even the baby continued to stretch and push against her in response to her unsettled state.

Low voices sounded from below, the heavy thud of the front door being pushed closed reaching her and she knew someone had been granted entrance.

Perrin.

Now it seemed she'd be examined, given the all clear, and then she'd have to face Galen. It wasn't something she was looking forward to, but it was necessary.

Masculine voices grew nearer, some entreating and some downright aggressive and she wondered if Galen had violated Perrin's orders. She'd been told that the pack doctor was above all others when it came to matters of health. Apparently not.

With a sigh, she slowly turned her body, dropping her feet to the floor, and uncurling herself in preparation of the doctor's entrance.

Except, when the door open, that's not to who met her gaze.

"Andrea."

The Alpha bitch smiled. "Good morning. How is *my* child?"

A low masculine gasp reached her and she met Leo's gaze over the woman's head. Fury filled his gaze, the expression directed at Andrea and then it flicked to Lissa. So many emotions filled his face, flickering from regret to fury and then he was gone. He whirled on his heel and stomped away. His level of anger made her wonder if he was finally realizing the type of male his Alpha truly was.

"*My* child is perfectly healthy," she countered.

"He's yours for now. We'll see how long that lasts."

Her son trembled within her womb, and she laid her hands across her stomach. "Forever. You intimidated me once, and I ran. But this time, you can be damn sure you are not getting your hands on this baby. Neither of you are."

"Like I said, we'll see." Andrea smirked.

No. It wasn't happening. Period. If denials didn't work with this woman, she could revert to the truth as Perrin explained it. "No matter my problems with Galen, I'm his mate and this is his child. He wouldn't hurt either of us."

Yellow eyes clashed with hers, Andrea's inner wolf making its presence known with that bright flare. The shape of Andrea's mouth changed, wolfen fangs pushing through her gums and she curled her lips to expose the deadly teeth. "No, but that doesn't mean I won't."

Andrea took a step farther into the room, and Lissa scanned the large space for some type of weapon. Andrea's wolf was close to the surface, and Lissa realized it was only a matter of time before the Alpha bitch attacked. Her only hope now was to stall and if that failed, hit Andrea hard enough to distract her while Lissa ran for help. No matter what problems swirled around her and lingered between her and Galen, he had issued orders for her care. She didn't imagine he was aware of Andrea's presence.

Unless he was.

She hated this fucking indecision, this unease and wavering beliefs in him.

"So what's your plan, Andrea?" Lissa eased toward the bed, particularly the bedside table. Maybe she could grab a lamp...

"You. Gone."

"And Galen is okay with this?" *Keep her talking. Keep her talking.*

"I told you before you ran, you stupid bitch. Galen and I are meant to be together. We're ruling this pack. I may not be his mate, but I am his equal. That baby is ours." The woman flexed her hands and fur erupted from her pores. "Make this easy on yourself. Don't fight."

Lissa clutched her stomach. "He won't live if you take him now."

Andrea bared her teeth with a growl. "I have a doctor who will ensure he lives and you... don't."

The Alpha bitch took another step toward her and Lissa reached for the bedside lamp, hand trembling as she fought to wrap her fingers around the decoration. "But there's still a risk to him."

"Stop delaying the inevitable."

"Do you really think Galen would want you to gamble with his son's life in such a way?"

Andrea smirked. "Who says he doesn't already know?"

A harsh, growling, snarling voice cut through their conversation. "I do."

Part of her may hate him, but she sighed in relief to see him framed in the bedroom doorway. "Galen."

Where Lissa whimpered in relief, Andrea purred. "Galen."

"Alpha," he snapped the correction. "Get the fuck away from my mate. Now."

"But Galen..." Andrea turned her attention to him fully and took a step in his direction. "We had plans—"

"Before I found my mate," he growled, the sound rolling and growing in volume with each passing heartbeat. "And you're why she ran. Aren't you?"

He took a step toward her and Andrea stiffened. "I told her what we'd discussed. That we would take the child of another—"

"Adopt, you crazy bitch. *Adopt*." He rolled his

shoulders, and fur sprouted and coated his neck and cheeks. "You almost cost me my family."

"No," she shook her head. "I'm your family. With the baby, we'll be..."

Andrea must have finally realized the truth, recognizing that Galen wasn't backing down from his aggressive stance. He wasn't attempting to console her or agree with her in any way.

"We'll..." her voice was thin and high-pitched, and Lissa watched as the disbelief rippled across her body. "We're... You said..."

Galen released a rapid whip of Greek, the words seeming to pierce the woman's heart.

"But—"

"But nothing! You may be an Alpha bitch, but not mine. No more." He launched into Greek once more and Andrea flinched as she dropped her gaze to the floor.

Lissa may have despised the woman, but it seemed as if Galen was grinding her beneath his boot heel. "Galen..." she eased away from the bed side table and took a step toward him. "Don't you think—"

"Don't you speak, you hairless bitch!" Andrea spun on her, gaze intent and hate filled her expression. "I'll—"

Then he was there, arm wrapped around Andrea's waist and bodily lifting her from the floor. The woman tried to shift, fur sprouting over her skin, arms and legs shortening and transforming, but a harsh word from Galen had the change halting in its tracks.

"Enough!" Galen shook her. "Enough." He hauled her to the bedroom door and tossed her into the hallway. She spied Leo and Stavros lurking nearby, and the men were quick to grasp their Alpha bitch. "Secure her and contact the Greece Alpha." The words were immediately followed by a howl from Andrea. "You do not speak! You are lucky you are breathing! You interfered with a mating and will be punished as such. Get her out of here."

He remained in place, even after the guards disappeared with the snarling Alpha bitch. He stood framed in the doorway, his broad shoulders tense. It wasn't until the barks and howls died down that he allowed himself to move. But it wasn't to come to her. No, his entire body slumped, his shoulders dropping and spine curling in. He took a deep breath as if he was preparing himself to face her, but yet he still remained in place.

He was... She didn't want to call him broken, he was too strong and fierce a man for something like this to shatter him. No, not broken, but cracked. Vulnerable. He took another of those deep breaths and finally straightened, turning toward her. Pure determination and unbendable steel filled his expression. The wolf was still near the surface with its sprinkling of fur and yellow eyes, and she could practically see his Greek pride wrapped around him in a cloak. This was the man she'd first met, the one who swept her off her feet and into his bed within twenty-four hours of meeting. He'd convinced her to spend her vacation with him with that fierce desire and overwhelming dominance. He'd bulldozed her, coddled her, cared for her with the sweetest touches and most passionate embraces. He made her fall in love with him the same way, and even as she ran, that love hadn't been truly banished.

And even what damage it suffered beneath Andrea's actions, it had been slowly repaired by the time they spent together. Those remaining dents and dings were filled when pure surprise coated his features at Andrea's words, and he was quick to tear her from their lives.

"You're not leaving. I thought I could be the bigger man and let you leave since you despise me so much. But that is impossible. You are staying." The words were firm and not to be denied. He was the Liakos pack Alpha at this moment. "You may hate me all you like, but you are mine. That child is mine." He crossed his arms over his chest. "I will not have my family outside my den."

"No—"

"*I will not let you go.*" He released a growl, curling his lip and exposing one elongated fang in a pure threat.

He didn't understand.

"If you would let me finish. I was saying that, *no* we won't be outside your den." Some of the tension left his body, but still he remained in place. Lissa took a step toward him, and then another, gradually lessening the distance between them. "As long as you tell me Andrea was lying. "

Shock filled his features. "Of course she was lying. A Greek male—an alpha—would never do such a thing to his woman."

His woman wasn't exactly a declaration.

"Am I your woman?"

Now he glared at her. "You have been since the moment I laid eyes on you, the moment I scented you." He huffed. "Why are we discussing this? You are my mate. This is done. There is nothing else to talk about."

She took another step forward. "What does that mean?"

"I do not know why you continue. You love me. I know this, so why do you fight?"

Lissa shook her head. She did love him, but not his

Greek pride that wouldn't let him say anything other than "mine." Or perhaps that was his wolf speaking. Or his business mind that never gave up on a deal. It was just her luck that she fell in love with a Greek werewolf tycoon.

"I want the words, Galen. Am I your woman? What does it mean to be your mate? Am I just a convenient broodmare who gets left out of your life?"

A low growl came from him, not of anger but frustration. He closed the distance between them in two giant strides, and then she was enveloped in his firm embrace. Despite her large belly, he managed to hold her close and snug against him. "You are the one for me. I will never desire another. I want no other. We will rule this pack together. I will have an Alpha bitch to control the female wolves, that cannot be avoided, but I only share myself with you. Is this what you needed to know?"

"Yes." It was everything to her. Everything she'd hoped for and she was afraid to let those hopes rise too high.

Galen grunted. "Good."

Any further conversation was silenced by someone's approach, and Perrin quickly filled the doorway his always-present bag in one hand. Worry coated his features, and he focused intently on Galen.

"What are you doing here? I told you to—"

"I know what you told me, but I could not stay away from my mate." Galen's eyes remained locked on her as he spoke to his brother. "Did you speak with Leo and Stavros?"

Perrin sighed and ran his free hand through his midnight hair. "Yes. An announcement will have to be made…"

"Yes, but not until I have properly cared for Lissa. Has the news spread of not only Andrea's incarceration, but also the joy of their Alpha joining with his mate?"

"Galen, I'm concerned that Melissa—"

She didn't know what was involved in an Alpha joining with his mate, but she wanted nothing more than to be with him in any way possible. She'd been stupid to listen to Andrea and not question Galen, to keep her mouth shut when Andrea abused her, but things were different now.

"Melissa is fine."

"Your words last night." Perrin reminded her.

"That was because of Andrea and her interference." She tilted to the side to meet Perrin's stare. "We're going to straighten things out, Perrin. We're going to talk."

Galen lowered his head and nuzzled her neck, lips against her ear. "We will do more than talk."

"I heard that," Perrin snapped. "If, and I mean *if,* Lissa feels up to it and only then."

Galen—her mate—growled anew and she rolled her eyes. "It's his job to look after me."

"That's *my* job."

A discreet cough sliced through their conversation and her mate turned his attention to the doorway once again to find Leo lingering. "Alpha?"

Lissa patted his chest. "Go take care of the pack. Perrin wanted to examine me and he will come give you a report as soon as he's done."

He brushed a soft kiss across her lips. "I do not wish to leave you—"

"But your pack needs you."

"And she needs rest." Perrin cut in again.

She received one last tender kiss, this one more firm than the last, but not nearly passionate enough for her tastes. "I will come to you when this is finished."

With that, he released her and strode toward the door, stopping only long enough to murmur a few words to Perrin. The doctor's cheeks flushed, but he nodded and then Galen truly was gone.

When Perrin was closer, she spoke. "What did he say?"

"He wanted to know if it was safe for you to do more than talk for he does not want his desires to hurt you."

She licked her lips, a different kind of tension thrumming through her. "And what did you say?"

More redness. "I said yes."

Perrin said yes, and Lissa... After all of this, with love still filling her heart, she wanted to say yes as well.

CHAPTER NINE

Lissa almost went to his room, snuck in and made herself at home, but she didn't have that much self-confidence. No, her courage abandoned her after her long, hot shower and then she slipped into her nightgown. It wasn't like what she'd worn for him before. The straps were not delicate thin strings and her breasts weren't cradled by intricately woven lace. Silk did not caress her skin. No, she was heavily pregnant, which meant comfortable cotton that was thin so she didn't get hot or constrict her movements.

She stared at herself in the mirror, looking at this tent of a nightgown that covered her, and wondered what Galen saw in her. She was... as big as a house. But when he looked at her with need in his eyes, she felt as she had when they met. Beautiful. Seductive. *Wanted*.

The question was, did he truly want her now? It'd been hours since she'd seen him, hours since the truth had been revealed and Galen stated he wanted her forever, in his bed and in his life. Even Perrin believed the same.

So why the doubts?

Because... She was as big as a house. And she'd hurt him. Andrea hadn't just battered Lissa's emotions, she'd torn their relationship in two. But Andrea wasn't the one who walked away, she was just the catalyst. If she'd only...

Trusted in him. Believed in him. Admitted her feelings and...

A soft click drew her attention, a delicate scrape of metal on metal that sounded distinctively as if someone had opened her bedroom door. She tore her gaze from the mirror and agonizing over her appearance to slip from the bathroom into the bedroom. The second her feet touched carpet, she froze in place, unable to move.

Galen had come to her. He was rumpled and appeared weary, but he was here. In her room. His slacks were wrinkled, his shirt was half unbuttoned and exposed his deeply tanned chest, and his tie hung loosely around his neck.

"Galen?"

He turned toward her and his expression immediately cleared, the exhaustion suddenly gone. "Melissa... My mate..."

He sighed and padded toward her. When he reached for her, she readily went into his embrace, turning slightly which allowed her to rest her head on his chest. Her arm went around his waist while he did the same to her. His free hand came to rest on her distended stomach, and she relaxed as he gently stroked her belly.

"How are you?" He pressed his lips to her temple in a soft kiss. "How is our little one?"

"Good." She lifted her head to meet his gaze. "How are you? How are things with the pack?"

"Better than last night, but not perfect."

She winced, knowing her part in the drama and problems now surrounding him. "I'm sorry."

"No. Never apologize for the trouble that woman caused." He carefully withdrew from her and gently gripped her by the shoulders. "Why did you not tell me everything? She injured you. Why did you not tell me that?"

"Does it matter?"

"Of course!"

Lissa sighed. "The first time she hurt me, Leo saw her do it, but she ordered him to remain silent. I went to you and tried to talk to you about it, but he wouldn't speak up and support me and you..." Self-loathing filled his expression and she was quick to continue. "It doesn't matter anymore."

"I have spoken with Leo. I have forgiven him. But I should've believed you."

"You didn't know me."

"I knew I loved you," the words were harsh and hoarse, but she didn't care about the tone. She simply cared about the message.

"Lov*ed*?" She was so very afraid to hope.

"Love. I still do. Even when I was an idiot and didn't see the truth. Even when you ran from me. I did not stop." He released her shoulders and stroked her cheek. "I will never stop, my mate."

Tears stung her eyes, and moisture blurred her vision. "I love you, too."

"I know this."

Cocky Greek. Cocky wolf.

But hers. All hers.

Silence wrapped around them, not a single hint of other sounds invading her space. The house was quiet, the staff remaining unobtrusive. With the truth of Andrea's actions came a new respect for her. While she had hoped they would forgive her and accept her for herself, she would take this thawing.

"Do you know how beautiful you are?" His fingertips glided along her jaw and down the delicate line of her neck. "Your skin is like silk and your lips taste like heaven. Being with you is what I live for. When you were gone..."

She placed two fingers over his lips. "I will never leave you again. I will learn to speak up and you will—"

"Believe in you without question. Never again will another come between us."

Their son chose that moment to shift and turn inside her and Galen chuckled. "Except this one." He dropped to his knees and pressed his mouth to her stomach. "Hello my little one, do not be so hard on your mama. Go to sleep now for papa. I must love your mama now."

A heated flash burned her cheeks when she understood what he said. "*Galen.*"

He rolled to his feet with a teasing grin on his lips. "Yes, *agapi mou*? You have need of me?" He grasped her fingers and drew her toward the bed. "Because I have need of you. I must make you mine."

Lissa pointed at her stomach. "This is a big sign that I am yours."

He shook his head. "No, not enough. Not for wolves." He stopped and brushed her hair behind her back, tracing the line of her neck and shoulder and only stopping where they met. "I would like to mark you here so all will know you are claimed."

She wanted that too, despite it involving his teeth going into her flesh. "Yes."

His eyes flared yellow, the wolf rushing forward and forcing his human teeth to turn into wolf fangs. "Now."

She nodded. "Now."

One moment she was standing in her room and in the next she was swept into his arms. He didn't seem bothered by her added weight in the slightest and within seconds, he was striding down the hallway toward his own room with long, sure steps. She leaned her head against his shoulder, holding him tightly as he navigated the house. She enjoyed the feeling of being in his arms once again, the strength and power he possessed, making her feel safe and protected.

When his scent didn't just fill her lungs, but also

consumed her body, she realized they'd entered his room. His presence was in every surface, every piece of furniture and decoration. The room was emblazoned with his aromas and she felt her body awakening. As if it were trained to respond to him in this space. Walking into his bedroom was like flipping a switch. Memories of their time within the four walls assaulted her, reminding her of the past and urging her to embrace the present.

The space was familiar and yet... different. Different in that the bed had been repositioned, no longer in the same place she remembered and now one wall seemed consumed by mirrors. Galen padded toward the king-size bed, easing them closer.

"What...?"

"For you." He carefully released her legs and gently lowered her to the ground. He kept his hands on her until he was sure she was steady.

She shot him a questioning glance. "What do you mean?"

"I cannot make love to you as we once did because of our son." He repositioned her, making her face the mirror while he slid behind her. "Like this, I can. I can fill you and touch you and still see your eyes as I bring you pleasure."

She shuddered with those words, her body already

reacting to each syllable. Her center heated and ached while her breasts grew heavy and nipples hardened. The firm tips were easily visible behind to the thin cotton of her nightgown.

"Already you respond to me." His hands abandoned her shoulders, sliding down the length of her arms, and then he reached around her to cup the large mounds. He gently kneaded her, thumbs stroking the tips and she trembled with desire. "Already you want me."

"Yes."

"Always." He lowered his head and she watched as he opened his mouth wide and placed his fangs at the juncture of her neck and shoulder. He didn't break the skin. He merely gave her a hint of what was to come and then released her. "Only ever me."

"Yes."

"Let me see you, *agapi mou*." He abandoned her breasts and reached for her nightgown, slowly inching it up her body and exposing her bare skin to his gaze.

"Galen..."

"You're as beautiful today as you were when I first saw you in the café. No, you are more beautiful. You are filled with our son. A fertile goddess."

She couldn't resist him and his web of words. So when

he tried again, she didn't make a sound as the cotton slid over her body. She was slowly exposed, the cloth caressing her and revealing her. A low rumble rose in his chest, the sound growing as more of her was revealed. She knew the sound, knew what it represented. He was anxious for her, his wolf desperate for her, and her belief was further confirmed by the press of his hardness at her back.

When he got to her stomach, she was unveiled in a rapid tug of fabric. It was as if the sight of her pregnant belly sent him over the edge.

"*Agapi mou...*" He reached around her once more, stroking her distended body. "Let me make you mine."

She had only one answer. "Yes."

Somehow she went from standing in front of him beside the bed to laying on her side on the soft surface with his nude body curled at her back. The long lines of his lean muscles conformed to her soft curves. The feel of his hardness against her bare skin sent a tendril of arousal through her. She wanted him now as much as she'd wanted him before. Even more so now. Her pregnancy had made her crave him with an urgency that almost frightened her.

He positioned her carefully, pillows in place to support her, support them both, and then he loved her in earnest.

Galen stroked her skin, teasing her breasts, caressing her stomach and sides before finally cupping the source of her pleasure. He slipped his fingers between her lower lips, teasing her moist flesh with an expert touch and sending her spiraling higher. She moved with him, careful shifts of her hips as she encouraged him to touch her where she needed most. He did the same, sliding his length against the globes of her ass as they took pleasure from each other.

And all the while their gazes remained locked in the mirror. She reveled in the appearance of his wolf, the brightness of his eyes and the sprinklings of gray fur that decorated his cheeks. He wanted her, both parts of him wanted her.

And she wanted him. She wanted to be his.

He continued tormenting her, circling her clit with the pads of his fingers, and driving her crazy with need. She rippled and tightened, anxious for his possession. She needed him. Desperately. She needed more than just his fingers and hot breath against her neck.

She ached to have him inside her with both his hardness and fangs.

"Please. Galen, please..."

"Tell me," he growled and she was unable to deny him.

"Make me yours. Please."

Once again he took control, easing her into a position that would give them both undeniable pleasure as he gently slid into her. He stretched her just as he had so many months ago, possessing her in a single, fluid thrust that consumed her.

She sighed when he was fully seated, the sound immediately followed by his satisfied purr. A wolf that purred.

From there, it became a careful, but no less passionate, slide of bodies. Of him thrusting in and out of her sheath, his hand still snug between her thighs and stroking her as he made love to her.

She catalogued each emotion that traversed his features, from love, to need, to a possessiveness that almost frightened her. But it couldn't frighten her. Every one of those emotions belonged to Galen. Her love. Her mate.

She panted and fought for breath with the rising tide of pleasure. Her only comfort was that he was in the same condition. His moist breath bathing her skin, his mouth hovering over the juncture of her neck and shoulder. His teeth were long and sharp and ready to pierce her.

"Galen..." she whined.

"You must come, *agapi mou*. For me."

She rippled around him, tightening and milking his intrusion as the first tremors of her release overtook her. With his words, she could do nothing but become a slave to the sensations. Pleasure like she'd never known, not even when they were first together, overwhelmed her. It consumed her in a blinding wave and she could do nothing but endure and embrace the sensations.

Distantly she recognized that Galen increased the pace of his lovemaking, making her ecstasy fly higher, and an echoing howl filled her ear. The sound was immediately followed by a sharp sting of pain that, rather than diminished her pleasure, magnified it. It sent another rushing orgasm through her, yanking yet another scream from her lips, his name bouncing off the walls of the room.

At that moment, he stilled. His hips no longer pumping in rhythmic thrusts and retreats. No, he was snug against her, his length throbbing within her core and she knew he'd found ultimate satisfaction as well.

They remained frozen in place, their bodies locked, until he gently withdrew his teeth and exposed the claiming bite. It was bloody, obviously, as well as purple and red with the damage he'd caused. And... beautiful.

He bathed the injury with his tongue, lapping up the

remaining droplets of blood while sealing the wound. When that was completed, he carefully withdrew his softened length, leaving her utterly empty and bereft.

But not for long. She was without his touch for hardly a moment before he had her repositioned, easing her from the edge of the bed and trading places so she was snug in his arms while still laying on her left side. It was a confusing game of musical beds, but he was quick to explain why.

"I read in the book that's pregnant mothers should not rest on their right side. I will rearrange the room so this is much easier next time."

She wiggled against him, allowing her stomach to rest on his side. "You read about this?"

"You are my mate and pregnant with my pup. I will always care for you as well as I can. This is a small thing." Arrogant Greek.

"And you think there will be a next time?"

Galen gently squeezed her. "I have you in my den." He brushed a kiss on her new wound. "My claiming bite on your shoulder." He lifted her left hand, running his fingers over hers. "Now I only need to put my ring on your finger and I will have everything," he murmured.

Her heart stuttered and then raced. "Was that a proposal?"

"No. A statement. You will wear my ring. No arguments." His words were solid and unbending and...

Perfect.

EPILOGUE

Stefano tumbled tail-over-head, running so fast his small puppy paws tripped over each other. By the time his small back landed on the pale sand, he was wearing his skin once again. No one had told her a werewolf toddler began shifting at such a young age. The first time she'd gone to his crib for a midnight feeding and found a whimpering fur covered wolf pup she screamed down the house.

Nearly all the males had come running, Galen leading the pack and immediately followed by both Leo and Stavros. The men had become little Stefano's godfathers, and Leo was now the first to offer to escort her wherever she had to go.

The moment he'd understood Andrea's machinations, he'd dropped to his knees with an apology for his behavior. Galen had ached to tear the man's throat out, but Lissa was touched by the man's loyalty to his Alpha. Now she couldn't go anywhere without him or Stavros tripping her up. Even now, both men lazed nearby, each of them wearing their fur as they rested in the shade of a large umbrella. If they were bound and determined to accompany her, they were going to at least be comfortable.

Her son quickly rolled to his feet, short legs moving a mile a minute as he raced over the sand. He shot toward the ocean, dropping to four feet as he struck the water line and bounced amongst the waves. The nanny was immediately at his side, scooping him into her arms and tossing the wriggling bundle in the air with a laugh. Now he released a few short barks and then howled with his happiness. She and Galen had made a beautiful child, quick to smile and extremely protective of those he loved just as he had been when she carried him for nine months.

"Papa!" Her son wiggled and the nanny immediately lowered him to the ground. The boy shot toward the steps that led from the top of the cliff down to their small beach. "Papa! Papa! Did you see?"

Lissa turned slightly in her comfortable chair and smiled when she spotted her mate—her husband—grasp their child and lift him high above his head. "I did see, *agoraki mou*." He tossed him up once again and then cuddled him close. "My fierce little wolf."

Galen's words had the same reaction as always. Stefano picked up a low growl and bared his small teeth at his father, nipping at his fingers. "I'm a big wolf. Mama, tell Papa I'm a big wolf."

Shaking her head, she smiled at her mate. Two years. Roughly two years since she'd run from him, been dragged back, and after removing Andrea from their lives, she'd given birth to this beautiful child.

And would soon have another. She placed her hand on her still flat stomach, internally smiling at the soft flutter that met her touch. "Of course you're a big wolf, only big wolves get to be big brothers."

~

Howls Romance
Classic romance... with a furry twist!

DID YOU ENJOY THIS HOWLS ROMANCE STORY?

If YES, check out the other books in the Howls Romance line!

http://howlsromance.com

THE BILLIONAIRE WEREWOLF'S WITCH EXCERPT

ALL THREE REPRESENTATIVES OF BAKER, SLATE & Cromwell looked as if they stared death in the eye.

In a way, they were.

The lawyers, a group of supposedly unbiased humans, wanted Grant Hemming's pack gone. Oh, he doubted the extermination of the Hemming pack was their idea, but he and his wolves would be extinct regardless of their intentions.

The vamps were up to something.

The pages in his hand still held the heavy, burnt scent of recent printing. The stench assaulted his sensitive nose and his wolf internally sneezed in an attempt to clear the stink. There were other fragrances and sounds within the conference room on which he needed to focus.

Like the sour tang of fear that clung to the man at his right. Or the musk of worry that draped over the woman to his left. He could also hear the low chatter of teeth emanating from the third man in the room.

At first glance, the documents spread before him appeared to contain exactly what had been discussed, yet...

Why the fear?

Why had the partners in the law firm sent peons instead of attending the important meeting themselves?

Grant shuffled the sheaf of paper together into a thin stack and placed it on the long, cherry wood conference table. He scanned the summary page the firm had prepared, searching for anything that would point to the reason for the humans' anxiety.

The man at his right dabbed his forehead with a handkerchief, wiping away the accumulated sweat. "Is everything in order, Mr. Hemming? It's essentially the same agreement your father had with Lucre Holdings."

Essentially. He just bet.

"It appears to be." *And appearances can be deceiving.*

The woman at his left presented him with a pen. The instrument vibrated in her trembling hand. "Would you like to go ahead and sign, sir?"

Grant had remained successful, and more importantly alive, over his two hundred years by listening to his gut, and he wasn't about to dismiss the warning feelings now. He paused a moment and looked out the floor-to-ceiling window to enjoy the evening sunset, the various shades of yellow, orange and purple that decorated the skyline. What would the night hold if he refused?

"Actually, I'd like to look this over tonight. I'll call Baker in the morning if I have any questions and I'll meet with the Lucre representatives tomorrow evening." He pushed away from the table and rose. The human at his right reached for the pages, and Grant snatched them from the table. "You wouldn't have a problem with me taking the time to review them, would you? Baker has spent years telling me that I shouldn't sign a contract without reading it first."

The stench of panic battered at his senses, the room filling with the odor until he wasn't sure he could stand to remain any longer. "N-n-no, sir."

The wolf paced within him, salivating at the thought of taking the weak, pesky humans down. They were trying to trick him in some way, lead him down a treacherous path that could harm the pack. The beast ached with the need to destroy the threat.

Had it not been for the fact that they were human, Grant would have let the wolf rule him. Happily.

"Good." He strode from the room, dispensing with any pleasantries. If he discovered his concern was unwarranted, he'd have his secretary send them his apologies and a gift basket.

But, based on his suspicions, he'd be giving them a quick visit to hell instead.

Striding from the conference room, he took the first breath of fear-free air he'd had in an hour.

The moment he stepped across the threshold one of his sentinels, Hagan, was at his side, matching him step for step. "Alpha."

"We've got a problem."

"Sir?" The wolf's booted feet thumped over the office's carpeted floor, the sound muffled by the plush surface.

Ever ready for conflict, Hagan was dressed in his typical uniform of black leathers and combat boots. He stood out like a sore thumb wherever they traveled, especially the headquarters of Hemming Industries, but the first time Grant had questioned him on his chosen attire, the larger wolf had quieted him with a few words.

"I can look pretty, and you can be dead. Or I can carry my own personal army beneath the leather. Pick one."

Grant had voted for the leather. Just because the

Hemming pack followed the old laws and refrained from dishonorable challenges, the rest of the world did not.

Which made sentinels an unfortunate necessity.

Pushing open the doors to his office, he went straight for his massive desk and slapped the contract onto the shining surface. The soft click of the doors signaled that he was alone with his sentinel, and he slumped into his cushioned chair.

Grant ran a hand through his hair, worries over the future of the pack rolling through his mind. "I need you to find me a lawyer."

"We have a lawyer. Several."

He glared at Hagan. "I need one that isn't going to bend over and take it if offered enough money."

The other wolf raised a single brow. "I thought we had that, already. We've been using the Baker firm for centuries. What's changed?"

"Damn it, Hagan." He hated being challenged.

"Damn it, Grant," the man replied in a droll voice.

"You're an ass."

"And until someone gets me outta my spot, I have that pleasure." Hagan smirked. "So, what the fuck has changed?" His sentinel flopped onto a nearby couch without waiting for an invitation and then he dug into his jacket until he raised a cigarette in triumph. "Knew I had one left."

"Your mate is gonna kick your ass when you get home." Grant focused on the contract before him.

"Ah, the joy of a mate." Hagan flicked his lighter and ignited the cigarette. "She only grumbles until I bend her over..."

The alpha rolled his eyes. "Go find me a lawyer, Hagan."

"You still haven't told me why." The cherry of the cigarette burned bright.

"Because it appears the vamps are trying to destroy us, and they're using this century's contract to do it."

THE LAST OF THE SECRETARIAL POOL HAD LEFT HALF AN hour before and Rachel enjoyed the bit of quiet. Especially since it let her focus on everything she hadn't gotten done earlier in the day. Because she was slow. Slooowww. God had not made her to be a secretary. Ever.

She checked over the calendar on her screen and shot

off a few emails, wincing as she realized she was notifying her bosses a smidge late about their eight A.M. meeting. Oops.

The ringing of her phone snagged her attention and she picked it up without checking the caller I.D. "Hemming Industries, Rachel speaking, how can I help you?"

"Rachel, dahling..."

She rolled her eyes. "Heya, Gigi."

"You're still at work."

Rachel snorted. "Since you called my office line, I think it'd be obvious. What's up?" She shot off another email. Another wince. She was supposed to have responded to that one by noon.

Oops. Again.

"So, we're having a thing on Friday. You, me and a pitcher or five of margaritas. Oh, and Pitch Perfect. We can pretend we're a cappella singers and join in. It will be a-ca-awesome!" Gigi loved that movie way too much. Way.

"Yes on getting together and the movie. No on the margaritas."

Gigi's heavy sigh came across the line. "Because it's too

many *points* or whatever. I don't understand why you're doing this whole dieting thing."

"It's not a diet—"

"It's a lifestyle. But why? Your doctor said you're a perfectly healthy fat chick."

"I know, but..." But her butt was starting to touch the arms on her office chair and her boobs were busting out of her tops. The things weren't even low cut, but *blam* there was the boobage. "I'd just like to trim down a little."

Or, at least enough for a guy to look at her more than once. She didn't expect drooling, but...

"I disagree, but I don't want to argue. So, Friday. I'll drink margaritas and you'll have rum and diet soda. You can swing that, right?"

Sometimes, even if the woman griped about Rachel's choices, she loved easygoing Gigi. "Yup. It's a deal. I'll even bring along something yummy for dinner and dessert."

"The pineapple angel food cake thingie? That's, like, the only thing I dig."

Rachel snorted. "Yeah, I'll bring that along." Movement in her peripheral vision grabbed her attention and she turned her head to find the biggest man she'd ever seen, clad in black leather, standing outside her cubicle. "Uh, Gigi, gotta cut it short. Someone just showed up."

Someone ginormous and very, hugely, almost pee-her-panties scary.

Rachel stared at the man before her, gaze traveling up his body (and up and up and...) until she finally settled on his face.

Not waiting for her friend to acknowledge her words, she dropped the handset into the cradle and gave the man her attention. She'd seen him around the office, trailing after the president of the company, and the sight of him always sent a tiny sliver of fear racing down her spine.

"Mr. Hemming needs your assistance with a contract. Follow me."

She gulped. Look, more fear. Even She-Ra would have been scared of this guy. "I'm not a lawyer."

"Today you are." His voice was deep and gravelly. Probably from the cigarette dangling from his lips. It most certainly was not because he might be a werewolf. She'd heard rumors, and her Great Aunt Petunia had clued her in on their characteristics.

"Let's go," he grumbled around his smoke.

Didn't he realize that Hemming Industries had a strict no-smoking policy? Even if the person had a habit before being hired, they were soon browbeaten into giving up the cancer sticks. Then again, he was probably too big and scary for anyone to nag him.

"But, I'm seriously, really not a lawyer. And it's past six. I'm just on my way out—"

She was hungry, damn it. She had a date with some Chubby Hubby ice cream and a pepperoni pizza. In that order. Didn't the guy realize that it was her order out slash cheat day? Once a month, she splurged and got take-out. With money being tight since she sent anything left over after bills to Great Aunt Petunia to help the woman get by, she cherished these days. Getting to toss her *not a diet* diet out the window was just a bonus. A big one.

A growl filled the air. An honest to God growl. And the man rolled his eyes. She'd seen the guy around the office, always walking two steps behind Mr. Hemming. Since Grant Hemming was the company's president and one of the top ten richest men in the world, she wasn't surprised that he had some sort of scary-as-hell, maybe-werewolf bodyguard.

She just hadn't expected the man to show up in her cubicle. Ever.

"I can't—"

The man, Hagan from what she recalled, took a drag then dropped his head back to stare at the ceiling, blowing the pale smoke into the air. "Look, Miss Riordan, I know that you normally don't handle these types of situations—"

"Never. I'm not a lawyer, so I've never pretended to be one. Not even on TV. I'm a secretary and only half-way decent, at that." She really didn't want to do whatever it was Hagan needed. What if she screwed up? She needed her job. Needed, needed with a capital need. Great Aunt Petunia couldn't survive on her fixed income and depended on what Rachel sent along.

Another growl, deeper than before, and his gaze focused on her. Did his brown eyes have a hint of amber? She hadn't noticed that before. Then again, he was gigantic, and it'd taken her a minute to get past his massive size when he'd first stepped into her six-foot-by-six-foot space. He looked to be taller than her cubicle was wide.

And very werewolf-y.

She should have never taken this job.

"Are you a law student or not?"

Rachel furrowed her brow. "Well, yes. I mean, I was. I haven't taken a class in a while, but—"

"Then, let's go." A large hand wrapped around her bicep and tugged her from her square haven.

"Hey! Just because you're bigger than me doesn't mean—"

"Yes, amazingly enough, it does. Let's go." He tugged again, and she realized that resistance was futile. She would be assimilated, er, dragged along against her will.

With a sigh, she followed along, allowing the man to lead her through the hamster-like trail that was the general secretarial pool. He led her down the twisting and turning path to the elevator, still keeping his grip in place during their ride to the top floor.

Hagan merely nodded at the secretary outside what she assumed was Mr. Hemming's office doors and then entered the space, not even bothering to knock.

"That's right, cancel the—" Mr. Hemming's attention turned to her for a brief moment, and he stiffened and paused in the middle of his sentence. "Cancel tonight's picnic. I've got a few loose ends to tie up. Reschedule for Friday." Without bothering to say good-bye, he hung up on the other speaker and gave them his entire focus. "Hagan?"

Was he growling too? Good lord, the eighth richest man in the world was probably a werewolf. She'd stumbled into an amber-colored nightmare of ginormous proportions. It was one thing if it'd been a single guy, but the president of the company... If the head of Hemming Industries was wolf-tastic, who knew how many he employed.

Wrenching her arm from Hagan's grasp, she put a bit of space between her and the guard. "Mr. Hemming..."

The man's gaze captured hers, his dark brown eyes seeming to lighten as she stared at him and his chest expanded when he took a deep breath. "You'll call me Grant." Then he zeroed in on the bodyguard. "Hagan?"

"This is Rachel Riordan. She's from downstairs and is pre-law. I figured she'd be as unbiased as they came." The large man shrugged. "It's not like she knows anything."

"Hey, I think I'm offended." See, she could pretend ignorance of the supernatural with the best of them.

Hagan flashed a grin in her direction before returning his attention to Mr. Hemm—Grant. "She's feisty."

"She's taken. And so are you." Another growl from Grant. No wonder the man had to resort to practically abducting her for help. He'd probably scared away everyone else. Except other wolves. If he was a wolf. "Leave us."

Plus, dude, taken? What the hell did he mean by that?

Hagan stiffened beside her. "Alph—Boss, I haven't checked her for weapons. Give me five minutes—"

She cut him off. "Um, I promise not to kill him? All I've got is a Bic pen." She dug in her pocket and presented it to the larger man. "See? I'm harmless."

"See? She's harmless." The deep voice drew her attention back to Grant as well as that wide, toothy smile. *My, what big teeth you have.* Maybe he just had a twisted dentist. "Go."

That single word had Hagan retreating and disappearing behind the heavy wood doors, shutting out the rest of the world...and shutting her in with Grant Hemming.

Rachel remained frozen near the entry, heart thumping against her ribcage as she imagined the reasons behind the summons. Okay, it couldn't be horrible. The man wouldn't fire her for being pre-law. Then again, she was more *ex*-pre-law than anything. After her parents' death...

And, please, dear God, don't let it be her witch-factor. Great Aunt Petunia had warned her about wolves (jury was still out on his werewolf-y status) and witches and...

She'd *said* no one could sniff out her witch-tastic-ness. She prayed the old woman had been telling the truth.

Silence encompassed the room and she kept her attention trained on the company's president, the man no longer intent on her, but rather, the papers on his desk. His inattention gave her the opportunity to observe him, drink in his features, the lines of his body and the air of power that surrounded him.

Every woman in the company, married or not, had the hots for Grant Hemming, billionaire non-playboy and fierce businessman. There'd never been a woman attached to the man's name, leaving many to speculate that he was either extremely picky...or gay.

Rachel prayed for picky since hey, if he were gay, it'd ruin her most satisfying nighttime fantasies.

Seconds passed, her heart rate slowing with every tick of the clock until she finally felt normal. Then he looked at her, stared with those dark amber eyes and it felt as if he'd delved into her soul.

The sight of him stole her breath. He was tall, but almost everyone was considered tall when compared to her five and a half feet. But Grant easily topped six feet and he had wide shoulders and a broad chest that tapered to a solid waist. She resolutely ignored his package, unwilling to imagine her boss's cock, and moved on to his muscular thighs.

But it was those eyes... Those eyes seemed to change color with every brief moment that passed. It was the eyes that kept her frozen. Eyes that finally made her ninety-nine percent sure she was facing a wolf. The one percent was simply pure hope that she was wrong in her assessment.

"Rachel?"

She blinked, pulling herself from her musings and she concentrated on giving her boss her full attention. "Yes?"

"I have a problem, and I hope you can help."

ABOUT THE AUTHOR

Ex-dance teacher, former accountant and erstwhile collectible doll salesperson, New York Times and USA Today bestselling author Celia Kyle now writes urban fantasy, science fiction (as Erin Tate), and paranormal romances for readers who:

1) Like super hunky heroes (they generally get furry)

2) Totally dig beautiful women (who have a few more curves than the average lady)

3) Love laughing in (and out of) bed.

It goes without saying that there's always a happily-ever-after for her characters, even if there are a few road bumps along the way.

Today she lives in Central Florida and writes full-time with the support of her loving husband and two finicky cats. (Who hate each other with a passion unrivaled. What's up with that?)

Find Celia on the web...

www.celiakyle.com
celia@celiakyle.me

71131770R00093